MW00777329

Still On Herring Cove Road
Hickory, Dickory, Death

A Novel

BOOK 2

OF THE HERRING COVE ROAD SERIES

MICHAEL KROFT

Fifth Edition

CHAPTER 1
Saturday Morning, March 19, 1977

With his elbows resting on the kitchen's green melamine table and his fists stretching the front page of the *Chronicle Herald* newspaper almost to its tearing point, he stared at the four words. He couldn't seem to pull his eyes from the headline screaming out so loud he didn't need his reading glasses resting halfway down his long hawkish nose. The old man didn't want to, but he had to read the columns below.

Just as he was forcing his reluctant eyes down to the left column, a child's voice flew down the hall and smacked the old man on both ears. "Avriel Allen Rosen!" With the child's footsteps following close behind, Avriel, or Av to the Dixons and Mr. Rosen to everyone else, quickly flipped the paper onto the table, headline down, and tried to force his mind from that morning's news.

A short, blond ten-year-old in dark-blue pajamas entered the kitchen with an exaggerated scowl on his face, and standing in front of the old man, he shot up his arms to reveal two twelve-inch fuzzy-bearded action figures in each hand, all wearing dresses. "Av, you see anything wrong with these? Huh, do ya?"

With a straight face, the old man said, "Good morning to you too, Dewey. They look fine to me, though they would be prettier if they were clean-shaven and let their hair grow out."

As an orange tabby came out from beneath the table and rubbed its body against his shins, Dewey smiled and said, "Hi, Sam," and looking at Avriel again, he switched back to his scolding tone. "You snuck into my room and put them in dresses!"

"You are welcome. It was not an easy task to get my tailor to make those. He asked too many questions and gave too many strange looks. I did try a set of Barbie clothes, but they were too tight, too provocative, and when I returned them with the excuse that they were too small, I received a strange look from the salesman, almost like the one you are giving me now."

"You said we stopped the pranks! I surrendered the time you sent me to school that Saturday... or was it a Sunday?"

"Saturday, and we called it a ceasefire," Avriel said, cracking a quick smile, which had become much more frequent since first meeting the boy nine months before. "The soldiers are more realistic now. They look as if they are putting on a play. During the war, we did that once or twice. There were few women to play the female roles, so some chaps had to wear dresses."

Dewey lowered his cross-dressing action figures and huffed in defeat. "*Weren't any*, not *were not any*!"

Avriel took a sip of his black coffee. "Right, got it. *Weren't any* for *were not any*. Now, what would you like for breakfast: cereal, bacon and eggs, porridge, or corned beef and cabbage?"

"Ha, ha," the boy laughed sarcastically. "Cereal... Puffed Wheat, I guess." Then turning around, he stomped back down the hall toward his bedroom. "I'm going to change them all back right now!"

"Right, but put their dresses away neatly. We don't want

2

them wrinkled when they decide to act out *Little Women*." With Dewey huffing loud enough for him to hear, he added, "And do not forget to wash your hands and face," and received another huff from the boy.

"It's *don't,* not *do not!* You talk like Spock, a British Spock! I'm going to get you back, you know!" Dewey yelled from his bedroom,

Avriel smiled again, but dropped it when his eyes returned to the paper.

As the two ate their cereal, Avriel asked, "So, what would you like to do today? I was thinking of visiting Ruthy... Mrs. Rosen, and then afterward, we could take a trip downtown."

"Cool. Can we see the movie *Freaky Friday*? Everyone's talking about it at school. It's supposed to be really, really funny."

"Sure."

"So, what's in the paper?" Dewey asked through a semi-full mouth. "You keep looking over at it. It's gotta be something interesting, right? So what is it?"

"It's *got to,* not *gotta*, and, yes, there's a story... a story about... about rezoning to allow the construction of several office towers in Fairview. I feel if they do that, they should also rename the area Poorview."

Dewey nodded his head, accepting the old man's use of a previous day's article to replace the one currently stressing him.

Around seven, as the sun was setting, the front door of the small bungalow opened and a young woman with long blonde hair and an opened long wool coat over a red one-piece outfit, which looked like a cross between a straight dress and a smock, entered the bungalow. "Hi, guys," she called out melancholically as she dropped a plastic grocery bag containing a pair of flat shoes at the door. Taking her coat off, she hung it in the narrow closet.

"Hi, Mommy!" Dewey shouted from behind the closed bathroom door down the hall.

Avriel laid his novel down on the coffee table. "Hi, Lisa," he said as he raised his tall, thin frame from the sofa and joined the young mother at the entrance. "How was your day?"

Lisa pulled off her winter boots. "Uh... it was... it was the same as every Saturday, nonstop from noon to five. Sorry to take so long. The errands took longer than I thought."

"It is no problem. It is never a problem."

"Av, I don't know what we'd do without you," she said, hugging her friend, who instinctively stiffened up, but only slightly compared to the first time she hugged him when he had stiffened up like a full-body sculpture. Releasing him, she added, "What a day. I feel so dirty. I've got to take a shower."

"Dewey is bathing with his G.I. Joes. He will probably be there for another fifteen minutes. Come, I have your supper warming in the oven."

"It's *he'll* for *he will*," Dewey shouted again from behind the closed bathroom door and followed it up with a laugh.

As the two walked into the kitchen, Lisa asked, "Don't his contraction corrections annoy you?"

"Not at all. He only gets on that kick when I'm at my worst. This morning I dressed his dolls in dresses."

Dewey shouted, "Action figures! Dolls are for girls!"

"Right, action figures," Avriel said louder than necessary so the boy wouldn't have to struggle to hear him.

"Barbie dresses? They fit them?"

Avriel shook his head. "No."

"Oh... okay. Did he retaliate yet?"

As if on cue, Sam walked into the kitchen sporting a baby-blue buttoned-up infant sweater with its hood hanging over much of his small head.

Lisa laughed. "That's so cute," she said, picking up the purring cat. "It must have taken him a while to find his old baby clothes. If anything, he's persistent. And look at Sam. He's so easygoing, wearing it without a care."

"Well, he wiggled out of the baby pants almost immediately."

Lisa laughed again. "But you left the sweater on?"

"He did not seem to mind... and it is winter for another few days."

With the cat pushing his semi-covered head up against her chin, Lisa asked, "What did you two do today?"

"We visited Ruthy, and afterward went downtown to see the *Freaky Friday*," Avriel told her as he put on an oven mitten and opened the stove. "It is a chicken casserole, overcooked chicken casserole. I was afraid I would undercook it."

"I'm sure it's good. Right now, I will eat anything."

As Avriel placed the dish in front of her and warned her it was hot, she unbuttoned the tiny sweater and relieved Sam of it. Joining her at the table, he handed her the cutlery and took a deep breath. "If you have not heard, I should tell you. There... there has been another one."

Gently placing Sam on the floor, she picked up the fork, forced it into a tough piece of chicken, and asked, "Another what?"

His voice lowered. "Yesterday... another child... further down Herring Cove Road. This time just past the Spryfield Mall."

Lisa's eyes widened, and she froze as she put the fork of chicken into her mouth

Dewey had stopped playing with his two scuba diving G.I. Joes and was putting in some effort to eavesdrop on the adults' conversation. He had heard his mother ask, "Again?" but couldn't make out much of what Avriel said. It was something about the day before, but he wasn't sure if someone's dog was dead, a child had buried something dead, or a dog had dug up something dead. Whatever it was, he was sure something was dead.

Not able to make out anything more, he returned to playing with his action figures.

CHAPTER 2
Greeneland

Inside the long, red-bricked two-story building of the Halifax
Police Department on Gottingen Street in The North End, one
of the city's two predominantly Black communities, was
Detective Greene's office, or Greeneland as those around him
referred to it. His office labeled Major Crimes was tucked
away at the back of the first floor where he had to walk a
labyrinth of cubicles with their short walls and confined spaces
making him feel he was in the land of dwarfs.

In his dark-blue suit, his wife's favorite, and a white shirt
with a loosened black tie, Greene sat at his desk, rubbing his
thin mustache with one hand while staring at several official
sheets of paper in the other. He squeezed his eyes shut,
admitted to himself he would soon have to wear reading
glasses, and placed the preliminary forensic report back into its
manila envelope. They would deliver the final report once the
toxicology results came in. Leaning forward, he arched his
back, stretching it while releasing a groan. Straightening up, he
looked over the notepad of chicken scratches that his boss
hated and occasionally commented that he should've been a
doctor, which always caused Greene to sardonically reply that
he hoped they didn't hire him for his penmanship.

In a few minutes, Greene expected to hear the comment

again. He had a meeting with the chief of police and together they would have to decide what to say at the press briefing to be delivered in just over an hour and a half. They would have to determine if Halifax had a potential serial killer preying on children, and it wasn't an easy conclusion to make. There were too many inconsistencies between the two murders to state it was the work of one person. Of course, no pattern was ever followed a hundred percent, and the two horrific murders just over six months apart in the small city were so rare it would force most to believe they were the actions of one person.

During his time in Halifax, he had only been involved in a few press briefings, and he dreaded them. He didn't appreciate the spotlight. Greene was naturally a shy man and didn't appreciate going outside his comfort zone, but he was good at playing the role of a detective. Having done it for almost eighteen years, he had the part down. He was great at asking questions and evaluating the answers but was uncomfortable being asked the questions and having to supply the answers.

Greene knew the chief didn't appreciate the spotlight either, but it was only an occasional requirement of his job. The briefings were scheduled only hours in advance and the stress caused by them, including the disruption to his daily routine that he stubbornly followed, caused the chief to become temperamental and sarcastic.

For this briefing, the chief could be thankful he had a specialized Homicide Department, a relatively recent creation. Almost four years earlier, the city had separated its Major Crimes Section into three units: Fraud, Narcotics, and Homicide, and divided its pool of detectives between the more common crimes of fraud and narcotics. However, for the Homicide Unit, it looked outside the department for a more experienced homicide detective.

Greene had been working homicide in Toronto when he

spotted the Halifax Police Department's employment posting pinned to the announcement board hanging above his unit's coffee machine. The position interested him, and for several days, he tossed the idea around in his head, weighing the pros and cons carefully before informing his wife, who was warm to the idea of moving to a smaller city. She expected less stress on her husband and, therefore, less on their relationship, and she expected him to work fewer extra hours, giving him more time with his family. The only negative was the distance from their families, but they could always fly out twice a year to visit them, making it a small price to pay for all the positives. Then acting on the career opportunity, Greene flew to Halifax three times for interviews, and six weeks after applying, he was offered the job. It paid less, but the intangible benefits to the Greene family far outweighed the pay drop.

Until now, Greene had a relatively straightforward job, even as a Homicide Unit of one. Since first taking the job, there had been an average of almost twenty-three questionable deaths per year, and about half of those were determined to be suicides. Most of the actual murders were spontaneous, the result of domestic violence and bar fights, and easily solved in a few days, usually labeled as manslaughter for easier and faster trials. The remaining ones, those that were premeditated, were mostly the result of the city's organized drug trade, and in those cases, the Narcotics Unit of six, or the six stooges as Greene silently referred to them because of their tendency not to take their job as seriously as he felt they should, assisted him. That left maybe two or three murders a year that required his sole investigating, and except for the two recent murders of children, Greene had closed every case within a month.

The two open cases stressed him, not only because he had no hard leads, but because they were children and, rightly so, made the national and international news. It was one thing to murder an adult, but to murder children was so beyond shocking that the public had become vocal about finding the killers, and Greene was feeling the added pressure.

For the umpteenth time that morning, the small, blinking red dome on his muted answering machine caught his attention. For the last two days, it was in a constant blink and at one point made him believe it was a glitch in the machine's electronics. Having to bring the reporters' inquiries to his boss, over the last few days he had brought several dozen from local, national, and international news agencies, which forced the reluctant chief to hold a press briefing that afternoon.

Playing the messages, Greene was thankful there were only two and put in some effort to write them down legibly. Finished, he grabbed the notepad, the manila envelope, and a file folder and left his office.

In his brown three-piece suit, looking more like a business executive than the head of the city's police department, the husky and balding Chief of Police was welcomed by several blinding flashbulbs as he entered the station's large briefing room from the back. With Greene and two uniformed officers following him, they stopped as the chief stiffly walked up to the podium separating him from the dozen reporters, laid a few sheets of paper on it, and cleared his throat.

"Thank you all for coming," he said as he glanced around the room while avoiding any prolonged eye contact with the reporters. "I'm well aware that the question on everyone's mind is whether these two murders of children within the Spryfield area over the last six months are related to one another, whether they are the actions of one or more people, and I can assure you the question has also been on the minds of every officer in this building." His eyes glanced down at his papers. "Without making this a long lesson on serial killers, here lays our problem with committing to the serial killer scenario. Besides the fact that two spread-out murders don't qualify, by definition, as serial killings, the most consistent aspect of a serial killer is how he commits the murders. Past serial killers... and current serial killers generally choose one of the four ways to kill and do it in a consistent and specific way, like the closed case of the Boston Strangler and the open cases of the Cincinnati Strangler and the Axe Man of New Orleans. The most common method is stabbing, second most common is strangulation, then there's bludgeoning, and lastly and less common, perhaps because of the attention-drawing noise it produces, is shooting."

Taking a second to pause, the chief glanced down at his papers again and cleared his throat.

"Another considerable consistency of serial killers is the disposal of the victims' bodies. Much like the method of killing, it's usually consistent, whether it's burial, dropping them into a river, disposing of them on the side of a highway, or burning them." He cleared his throat again. "Without going into too much detail, these two victims have been murdered inconsistently, and each has been disposed of in different manners. Now, with nothing else to lead us to believe they're the work of the same person, we feel the press crediting the murders to a serial killer, which you... they have labeled the Kid Killer, is premature. Please keep in mind that murder investigations are handled differently for individual murders than for serial murders. We do not want to fall into the trap of looking for one killer when there could be two or more unconnected to one another.

"Now with that said, just to be on the safe side, even with no strong sign that the murders are the work of one person, such as a note or a signature element left at the scene, I... we should add that it would be prudent for all children to be accompanied by a parent or in groups when outside the home during the evening. I say this because each victim was alone when they disappeared.

"Okay, that's all we have for now. As more information becomes available, we'll let you know as we know. Now we have time for a couple of questions, and we'll answer them as best we can," he said, causing a bombardment of questions to rise from the small group of reporters.

"Yes, John. What's your question?" he asked, making eye contact with a heavyset, thick-mustached reporter from the *Chronicle Herald*.

"Thank you. Sir, do you have any suspects in either case?"

"Yes, we have several, and it would be premature to publicize their names at this time."

With hands flying up, the reporters launched a second bombardment of questions.

"Yes, Robert."

"Thank you. Do you know how long the last body rested before it was discovered, and can you tell us how the children were murdered?"

"At this time, we will *not* be disclosing the cause of the deaths and will say only that they weren't consistent, nor will we confirm any rumors. Regarding the first question, Forensics believes the second body rested for four days before being discovered, making the date of death March fourteenth. I should add that bodies in the small plots of forest in Spryfield are easily discoverable. They tend to be high-traffic areas, often used as shortcuts between the streets, as hunting grounds for BB gun warriors, and even as... well... places for young romance."

Several reports chuckled at the police chief's last words, giving a reporter unfamiliar to the chief time to get his hand up first.

The chief pointed to him. "Yes, your question?"

"Thank you. Henry Davis from the *Toronto Star*. Sir, with the first killing, you had charged a Ralph Walters with second-degree murder, but you later dropped the charges without a detailed statement, saying only that Walters was no longer a suspect. Can you elaborate on that, especially now that a second killing has occurred?"

The chief cleared his throat. "Yes, that's correct. We dropped the charges against Walters... Mr. Walters. I can tell you without any hesitation that he was not involved in the first murder... or this latest one. We had arrested him because of his close contact with the first victim and his claimed whereabouts on the evening of the child's death proved false." To take a moment to think, he pretended to scan his notes. "After Mr. Walters realized the spot he was in wasn't going to fix itself, he provided a substantiated alibi. His whereabouts on the night of the murder were certainly *not* illegal, though embarrassing." Then with his face revealing he had said too much, he cleared his throat again and said, "That's all I can say without dragging the innocent Mr. Walters through the mud any further. The charges against him have been dropped, and his name shouldn't be brought up again regarding the first murder case or the second. Okay, let's move on. One more question."

An older woman in a dark dress suit took a step forward and asked in a demanding tone, "Chief Henderson, what do you have to say regarding the rumors that because of the social class of the victims, they being from the poorer area, your department isn't doing all it can to solve these cases?"

Flushing red, the chief fought to control his voice. "Well... well, I never heard those rumors, but I will say we're certainly doing all we possibly can... possibly can do to find the killers of these children. They are victims... irrelevant of their social class. I'm not sure where these rumors are coming from, but there is absolutely no truth... no truth whatsoever to them."

As another bombardment of questions started up, the chief grabbed his papers from the podium. "That's all the time we have for now. Thank you."

Waving, he left the room with Greene and the two officers following him.

"I hate this shit!" he whispered back to Greene. "We need to solve these yesterday!"

CHAPTER 3
Eagerness and Anxiousness

Neither a bird sang nor a squirrel clicked, and even the wind seemed to hold its breath so as not to cause any branches to creak or brush together. The only sound was that of a shovel cutting into a pile of loose dirt and dropping it on a bedsheet-wrapped object resting in an almost four-foot-long rectangular hole. As it was slowly covered, it moved, squirming calmly at first as if just waking up, and then with the accompaniment of several childlike groans, it wiggled excitedly. Then like a butterfly escaping from its cocoon, the impression of its limbs became visible, and with the dirt continuing to fall, the sheet ripped at one end, exposing blond hair. As small fingers struggled to rip it further, a tiny nose appeared before a head broke through and a wide-eyed Dewey shook off the dirt falling on his head and screamed, "AV, HELP ME!"

Avriel shot up from the bed and stared into the semi-darkness. After realizing where he was, he wiped the perspiration from his forehead and looked over at Sam, who was looking back at him while lying on a white towel spread out on the other side of the bed. The curious animal stood up, stretched its back, stretched its front legs, and then stretched each hind leg before walking over to him and standing with his two front paws against the thin, pajama-covered chest to rub his furry face against Avriel's coarse whiskers, calming the old man who reciprocated by patting him.

After taking a few seconds to collect himself, Avriel lifted the heavy metal alarm clock from the nightstand and turned it at an angle so the streetlight's rays trespassing through the open curtains exposed the position of its thick arms. It was four forty-something, almost an hour before Sam would normally wake him.

Avriel considered going back to sleep, but his fear of the nightmare returning persuaded him not to. Laying the clock back on the nightstand, he scooped Sam up with one hand and with the other, pulled the sheets aside and got out of bed.

With Sam curled up and purring on his lap, Avriel sat at his small oak kitchen table, pondering where the nightmare came from. He was certain it was related to the news of the second child's death but wondered why it included Dewey. Perhaps it was a fear of losing the boy whom his wife had befriended and then forced onto the then much more socially awkward old man. The boy who had broken the old man out of his introverted shell, allowing him to live life after entering what should've been a very lonely retirement and whom Avriel couldn't imagine his life without.

Trying to pacify himself, he told himself it was a semi-irrational fear since Dewey was rarely outside alone to be placed in any danger, but he would make it an absolutely irrational fear by making sure his little friend was never alone.

Then the subtle scent of his wife's favorite perfume soothed him. He might have tried to confirm the scent's presence by a long sniff, but after trying and failing several times before then, he had learned not to bother. It was never there long enough for a second take. Since first experiencing the mysterious wave of the scent, Avriel had assumed it resulted from a need to hold on to something from his wife, and he came to believe it when after several months of smelling it, he found the bottle of perfume and tested it in the air. Surprisingly, it wasn't the same scent. The scent that snuck up on him and then vanished as quickly as it had come wasn't the perfume's straight-from-the-bottle scent, but the scent from it off of her neck — the more intimate scent.

Expecting his day could only go up from there, he took his first sip of that morning's black coffee, which eight months earlier Lisa had taught him how to make properly.

**

Lisa had arrived home from work just after three-thirty, and while she prepared supper, Avriel and Dewey worked at the newspaper-covered kitchen table putting together a model fighter jet. Normally the glue's odor didn't bother her, but that afternoon it seemed to be trying her patience and to make its mission easier, where cooking normally relaxed her, it didn't that afternoon. And before she had finished making supper, she gave up on trying to act happy in the hope of it becoming a reality. All she could do was fight not to feel any worse.

As the three finished a strangely quiet supper, Lisa asked Dewey and Avriel to leave the dishes on the table. "I–I have something to tell you two, and I can't think of any good way to say it, so I'll just come out with it," and with her son and her friend then looking curiously at her, she said, "Tomorrow or the next day, there'll be a for-sale sign on the lawn. It's not by choice. I've had to accept that I'll soon have a hard time making the mortgage payments." Trying to be strong, she looked at Avriel and fought back her tears. "It's either sell now or be foreclosed on later. I looked at all the options, including renting the house and re-mortgaging it, and selling it is the best one... but I'll have to try and rent it until then. The sales agent tells me it's a buyer's market, so it may not sell for some time, but... but the rental income should cover the mortgage with a little left over." Moving her eyes to a wide-eyed Dewey, she added, "We'll be moving to an apartment further down Herring Cove Road, about a mile past the Spryfield Mall. It's close to my work and your new school." With Avriel and Dewey shocked silent, it appeared to the young mother that the sudden news affected Avriel much worse than her son, whose mouth had dropped open and whose eyes seemed to twinkle with excitement. "So... so, what do you... what do you men think?"

"When will we be moving?" Dewey asked excitedly. "Are there other kids my age on the street? Where's my new school? Are we moving into a high apartment building, like the two on top of Cowie Hill?"

Lisa forced a smile. "We're moving in two weeks, and I've arranged a week's vacation for it. And I saw a few boys on the street who could be your age," she said, glancing at a glossy-eyed Avriel whose mind appeared to have left the conversation. "Uh... the school's just past work, so I can walk you to school in the mornings. And the apartment building's nothing special. It only has three floors."

Dewey's smile flipped to a frown. He thought it would've been fun to look down from high above. Maybe he could've even dropped a G.I. Joe in a homemade parachute from his bedroom window to watch it slowly descend to Avriel waiting below. But the height of the apartment wasn't a deal-breaker. He could still make new friends and could reinvent himself in the new neighborhood and at a new school. He could be a kid on the street instead of a *little* kid on the street.

Dewey was about to ask if he would have to start the school year over at the new school when Lisa said, "Av... Av, you can sleep in now instead of having to get up early to take Dewey to school."

Avriel had failed to hear Dewey's questions and Lisa's responses, and he even failed to realize they were moving to the area where the second murdered child was found. A thick anxiety had wrapped itself around him, causing his heart to beat hard and breathing to become difficult. Hearing his name, he cut through the anxiety and took a deep breath. "What... what does it mean regarding us?" he asked, and then embarrassed for asking, blushed and then blushed more when he realized he was blushing.

Reaching over and squeezing his forearm, Lisa caused him to blush even more. "Nothing's going to change. Maybe I'm being selfish, but I... we still want and need you. We're only a ten-minute drive from each other... if that. Av, the three of us are a family, and nothing's going to change that, nothing. I can't even imagine my world without you."

Avriel's question surprised Dewey, who added, "Yeah—"

"Yes," his mother corrected him.

"Yes, you're our best buddy. We'll always be there for each other. That's what you told me best buddies do. Remember?"

With the anxiety trying to cover him again, Avriel said, "Yes... yes, I did. I... I suppose the surprise of the news made me a bit anxious. It has been a while since I experienced that. I almost did not recognize it."

Dewey smiled. "It's *didn't,* not—"

"Dwight Dixon, that's getting old!" his mother scolded him.

**

Dewey was too excited by the news of the coming move to sleep. Resting on his side with his head sticking out from the Spiderman blanket, he stared into the dark as he considered how his life could change for the better. He had never lived in an apartment, but except for its elevation, he didn't consider it much different from a house. There should be all the same rooms as his house, so what would that change? At the new location, he could make friends with boys his age who would want to be around him. He had never had that on Gilmore Street where he lived all of his short life and where there was no one his age to hang out with, making no one to hang out with since he didn't enjoy hanging out with the younger boys and the older boys felt the same way. And then there were his classmates. On Gilmore, he never saw his classmates outside of school. They either lived along the townhouse-busy Cowie Hill on the other side of Herring Cove Road, which he wasn't allowed to cross, or they lived on his side but more than a few streets away from him, too far for him to go to alone. Would he miss his classmates? Would they miss him? He thought not. They were more like boys he knew *of* rather than boys he knew. Maybe that's why they're called classmates and not classfriends. At the new school, he hoped he could turn some classmates into friends and walk to and from school with them, just as he had seen other boys doing on his and Avriel's walk to and from his school. The way Dewey then saw it, when it came to having friends, the new place could only be better than where he was.

Eventually, after several times thinking about his new home, new school, and potential new friends, his excitement lost to fatigue and he fell asleep.

**

Avriel struggled to sleep. With Sam snoring beside him, he rested on his back with his arms by his sides and looked up at the ceiling. He couldn't budge his mind from the coming move and the potentially negative impact it could have on his relationship with the Dixons. He had to accept that the move was out of his control and all he could do was wait and see what would happen, but he could still worry about it. Lisa and Dewey were his family, not by blood, where the bond was automatic, but by love, where the bond was by choice. He needed them, and they needed him. They depended on him and he depended on them depending on him. They gave him a reason to get up every morning. They gave him a reason to exist contentedly, even to laugh occasionally, but all that could change. They were only moving two miles away, but the difference of not being directly next door couldn't be good for their relationship. Would Lisa find a babysitter in the new building? Would she call or would he have to do all the calling, as people tend to do when their friendship isn't equally reciprocated? Would Dewey and him grow apart as Dewey became familiar with his new surroundings? Then when the thought dove into his head to rent an apartment in the same building, he rejected it since it could be seen as rather pathetic, but he did ask himself that when they moved from Gilmore Street, should he move from it too? He told himself that at some point, he would have to move. Without them there, there was no reason for him to be on Gilmore Street that was now as cold to him as he initially was to it, and a month earlier, he was surprised to discover one reason for the tension when Mrs. O'Brien, a large woman who wore four-inch heels with her various muumuus, had quickly berated him for what she must have suspected was an affair between him and Lisa. "You should be ashamed of yourself! You being over twice her age!" she yelled from the rolled-down passenger window while her husband stared straight ahead as he drove past Avriel shoveling snow from his and Lisa's sections of the sidewalk. Avriel never mentioned his revelation to Lisa. She was too busy to notice their neighbors alienating them and it would've only added to her stress if she had.

Why wouldn't Lisa tell me sooner, Avriel asked himself, before realizing that had he known, he would've tried to throw money at her problem. He expected she knew that, and with his offer going against her recent independence, she must have purposely had the real estate agent come to her house when he and Dewey were out. It hurt that she would've gone out of her way to keep the move from him, but he accepted why she did it.

Then it occurred to the old man that his friends would be moving into the area where the most recent victim was discovered, and his heart raced. Fighting to relax, he filled his mind with happy thoughts of his and his wife's past together, and ten minutes later, just before sleep hit him, he was comforted by the fleeting scent of her perfume.

**

For the sixth night in a row, Lisa had a difficult time sleeping. All seemed fine the previous Saturday when she had committed to the apartment by signing the yearly lease, but it was a case of bad timing. She had only learned hours later that the body of a second child was discovered a half-mile away from the apartment. If she had known before then, she would've looked for an apartment in The North End, the other least expensive section of the city.

To add to the young mother's stress, she felt bad for causing Avriel stress that evening. She knew he didn't accept change well and he would've realized the apartment was in the area of the latest murder, but it couldn't be helped. It wasn't an impulsive decision. She had been trying to deal with the problem for weeks. There was no financial compensation for her estranged husband's recent death; in fact, the funeral home's expenses could've caused her to lose her house sooner if Avriel wasn't there. He was there before her estranged husband's death, and he was there for them immediately after, insisting on arranging and paying for the cremation that she would've stubbornly pushed back on his paying for if she hadn't been so shocked by the death and then taken aback by his firm insistence, which was so out of character for him.

Lisa would've cried herself to sleep that night too, but knowing Avriel would be there for both her and Dewey comforted her, and before falling asleep, she reflected on the irony of the situation. Once, during one of her and Ruth's many conversations, Ruth had asked her to watch over Avriel if she passed away before him, and partly because she believed Ruth could've outlived them both, Lisa had easily agreed to her request. And yet, immediately after Ruth's death, Avriel was watching over her and Dewey and had continued doing so since.

CHAPTER 4
The Move

The next day at school, Dewey informed his classmates he was moving and changing schools. When hearing where, one of his classmates warned him about Carson Street, where a lot of Black people lived, but that only excited Dewey, who thought it would be cool to have a Black friend. He was also warned about the Thirteenth Tribe motorcycle club's clubhouse being there, but he didn't understand what was so bad about a clubhouse. He was told there were a lot of poor families living there and was told by another boy that his parents called it the land of divorcees. Dewey didn't know what divorcees were but expected them to be something like fairies and was sure the boy's parents were just being silly. But he was concerned that he may be poor, and when he asked Avriel, the answer was an immediate, "No."

Relieved, he asked, "Are you poor?"

"I... I am not sure. I will have to check with my money manager and get back to you on that."

"Okay," Dewey said, nodding his head.

With the excitement of a child, Dewey counted down the days to the move, and as the first few passed, he pulled several pranks on Avriel, starting with turning the old man's spring jacket inside out, but Avriel didn't bring attention to it, which was his modus operandi, and he wore it like that for several days before it mysteriously changed to inside in again.

Unlike the past times, that prank and the few others Dewey pulled on his friend weren't returned in kind, and the boy only gave up on them after pulling a failed prank with Avriel's sandwich. The old man liked his egg sandwich layered in the order of cheese, egg salad, and lettuce, so Dewey proudly put it together in reverse, and when the old man noticed, he simply turned it over, oblivious to it being a prank. After that, Dewey was out of ideas, which didn't concern him too much since they were less fun when going only one way.

By the time the countdown reached three days, Dewey had carefully packed his things into the cardboard boxes his mother had flattened out and lugged home from work by bus, and he had proudly labeled each with a black marker. Initially, he had wrapped his model jets in newspaper and placed each in its own box, but when Avriel questioned the more than a dozen large boxes that the boy had labeled *Jets*, Dewey ended up repacking them into only two.

**

With it being the first of April, neither Avriel nor Lisa was in the mood for April Fools' Day jokes or pranks, so neither made any, and Dewey didn't make any either. With the excitement of the day's move, its traditional significance was lost on him.

Behind the steering wheel of his large black Cadillac and wearing a dark-blue spring jacket over his blue coveralls marked by several dark-green paint stains, Avriel followed behind the five-ton moving truck.

At the start of their drive to the new apartment, Lisa failed to hold back her tears, and Avriel pretended not to notice.

Nothing he could do or say could make her feel any better. Several times while boxing up her things, he had noticed her watery eyes, and he tried to ease her emotional strain by boxing up items while she was at work, but it didn't help. When she returned home and saw the additional packed boxes, her eyes watered again.

Oblivious to his mother's state and with his spring jacket over his coveralls, Dewey sat in the back holding his half-filled fishbowl containing his goldfish, Jacques Cousteau II. Looking intensely from one side window to the other, he watched as they passed a short strip mall on the left and a MacDonald's restaurant on the right, both familiar to the boy, before stopping next to the square brown-bricked building of King's Bar, and on the other side of the intersection, the stretched out Spryfield Mall with a large asphalt field of cars in front and several long mountains of snow melting along its edges. Seconds later, the lights changed, and they continued along Herring Cove Road as it swung down and to the left, a new frontier for Dewey who found it curious how that section of the road had only one sidewalk. The cement sidewalk remained on the left while gravel replaced the one on the right, and it interested him that people were walking on both sides, especially since he knew his mother would insist on him walking only on the cement side.

As the collar of his coveralls began to chafe his neck, he continued to take in everything they passed on both sides, though nothing stood out to warrant his excitement or justify the irritation. On the left side, they passed a fenced-in school, which later that night he would learn was his new school, and it was followed by a grocery store, which he assumed correctly was where his mother worked.

When Dewey broke the silence by asking why there was mostly forest on the right, Avriel told him a creek called the

MacIntosh Runs flowed along that side just behind the trees, causing Dewey to laugh before asking if another creek had already taken the name MacIntosh Diarrhea. Avriel laughed a rare belly laugh, and his mother cracked a slight smile.

Further down on the left, they passed a line of older wooden houses with overgrown lawns, and replacing the forest on the right was a hill lined with several streets of single-story houses. After passing a red-bricked corner store on the left with the words *Green Gables* displayed prominently above its door, they passed on the right, a curiously steep road that twisted left at the top to disappear behind the hill of trees. Dewey only got a glimpse of it, but a glimpse was all he needed to think about how scary it would be to ride down it on a bicycle, especially in the rain.

Driving two more blocks, following the forest on the right as they passed a dozen older wooden houses on the left, the moving truck signaled left as it slowed to a stop. After waiting for several cars to fly by in the opposite direction, Avriel followed the truck as it turned onto a gravel street, where Dewey read the words *Autumn Drive* followed by a no-exit sign.

Making their way slowly down the drive, Dewey couldn't help but compare it to Gilmore Street. Instead of Gilmore's mixture of two-story and bungalow homes with immaculate front lawns, they passed on both sides an assortment of older wooden houses and narrow triplexes, all with front lawns of gravel. It was the first residential street Dewey came across that didn't have even one sidewalk.

As Avriel followed the truck to where the gravel road ended at the edge of a forest, Lisa pointed out the obvious apartment building to the right, a long orange-bricked three-story building with three rows of large windows starting from the ground up, and doing as she asked, he parked the car a couple of feet from a window of the building in a parking spot marked by a large eight painted between its white dividing lines.

After the three had watched the truck reverse up to the building's steps of one solid piece of concrete, Lisa, somewhat composed and with her keys in hand, took the fish bowl from Dewey, got out of the car, and walked quickly to the building's lobby to unlock its inside door for the movers.

With its engine off, Dewey followed Avriel out of the car to lean back against its fender and watch a tall, husky mover wedge a piece of wood under the glass entrance door to keep it open, and when two other movers opened the back of the truck, the three began carrying in Lisa's large collection of plants.

"Last in, first out," Avriel said.

"Except for us," Dewey frowned.

Avriel nodded. "Looks like it may rain."

"Feels like it may snow."

"True, it could."

Before that day's unusual chill had a chance to affect them, Avriel and Dewey were back in the car with its engine running, and as they listened to the radio's soft rock music, Dewey watched several boys dodging the movers to enter or leave the building, and as each passed the back of the car, Dewey pointed them out to Avriel with comments of, "Too young," or, "Too old."

After several minutes, Avriel said, "Old enough," and pointed out two boys standing on the other side of the gravel road with their arms crossed as they tried to keep warm while watching the movers.

Excited, Dewey turned around and watched the taller of the two with wavy red hair speak to the smaller boy with blond hair down to his shoulders, and when the smaller boy responded by speaking directly into the tilted-down ear of the redhead, Dewey assumed the taller one had a problem with his hearing.

With nothing to keep their attention on the two boys, Avriel and Dewey played Twenty Questions, and fifteen minutes into it and worrying he was about to lose a fourth game, Dewey was about to ask his sixteenth question when a knock on the driver's side window startled him.

After Avriel rolled down his window, the redheaded boy asked, "Are you folks moving in?"

"We are... well, he is. My friend Dewey is moving in."

"I'm Blue," the redhead said and then pointed his thumb at his blond friend beside him. "And this is Stevie."

Stevie gave a quick wave of his hand.

"It is a pleasure to meet you two. I am Mr... I am Avriel," he said, and then gestured to Dewey to introduce himself.

Taking his cue, Dewey almost shouted, "Hi! I'm Dewey!"

Moving their heads around Avriel to look at Dewey, Blue said, "Hi, Dewey. Welcome to the neighborhood. If you two have any questions about the place, I'm in apartment two. Nice meeting you, sir, and you too, Dewey."

Before Avriel or Dewey could respond, the two boys turned away to walk toward the building's entrance, where they dodged the movers before disappearing inside.

Turning to Dewey, Avriel said, "Blue? I would have expected him to be called Red. Rather a strange name, no? I have never heard that one before, have you?"

"I've heard of Violet and... and Little Boy Blue. Hey, you know what? Last summer, I saw those two on Gilmore Street! They were running with Robby the day before he got his two—" Dewey cut his words short as if something suddenly occurred to him, and Avriel was going to ask him what Robby got two of when the boy pointed toward the front of the car and exclaimed, "There's Mommy!"

Through the ground-level window in front of the car, the old man saw Lisa swinging her arms about as she directed the movers. "We had better put up curtains."

Disappointed, Dewey agreed. He had looked forward to being able to look down onto the street, if only from a couple of floors, but he never expected to be looking up at it through parked cars.

Avriel and Dewey played Twenty Questions until the movers were closing up the truck and Dewey was protesting his loss, and when they left the warmth of the car, he was complaining that he would've guessed earlier if he knew they could've used the same thing again, but Avriel put an end to it by telling the boy he had never read in any book, not even a law book, where it had to be a different thing each time.

Opening the trunk, Avriel handed a frustrated Dewey a gallon of paint, grabbed the metal wire handles of two more gallons, and left the rollers, brushes, and old bedsheets for the next day.

Cold and eager to see what the apartment looked like from the inside, the two hurried to the entrance to enter the building's lobby, and with the inside glass door locked, Avriel had to use the dented stainless steel intercom on the lobby's wall. Leaning his head back so he could make out the numbers on the small rectangular plastic buttons, Avriel found the one marked with a faded number eight and pressed it, making an uncomfortable buzzing sound much like that used by a game show in response to a wrong answer. Seconds later, a crackle came over the intercom. "Av and Dewey," he said to the wall before a louder buzzing startled them. Avriel was the first to recover and with his free hand, quickly grabbed the metal door handle, pulling the door open just before the obnoxious sound ended. "Uh... Dewey, when you have to get in, your apartment is number eight."

Carrying his can of paint with both hands, Dewey followed behind Avriel descending the flight of metal stairs to the first floor's stained carpeted hallway that was dimly lit by four of its six lights and where a strong, unpleasant smell filled their nostrils and a mêlée of sounds filled their ears: two televisions on two different channels blaring away, a dog yelping, two men loudly arguing, and an infant crying.

Near the far end of the hall, Avriel stopped at the last door on their right, directly across from another flight of metal stairs, which he would later learn led to parking at the back of the building. Opening the door, he stepped to the side, and with his free arm extended toward the apartment, bowed and said, "Your castle, My Lord."

As Dewey stepped through the threshold, a different unpleasant smell filled his nostrils just as the apartment's small size shocked him. To the right was a hallway and down it, on its left, were two opened doors. At the end of it was another opened door, revealing a white porcelain sink held up at its front corners by two chrome metal poles, and beside the sink, a toilet missing its cover. To the boy, the most bizarre thing was the narrow kitchen directly across from the entrance. It was only the size of his mother's walk-in closet and had about three feet of counter space on the right between the fridge and sink. And to the left, was a curious open space that appeared to act as both a living and a dining room, if only because the movers had placed the living room furniture at the far end and the dining room table and its chairs nearer to the kitchen.

With his large, thin hand on the boy's shoulder, Avriel stood behind him, almost expecting him to faint, and once confident his little friend was steady on his feet, he took Dewey's can of paint and placed the three cans to the left of the door.

"Hello, gentlemen!" a much better composed Lisa greeted the two, hugging and kissing each on the cheek before closing the door behind them. "Okay, Dewey, I had the movers put your stuff in your room. Your job is to unpack and set up everything you can. Av, could you help me unpack the kitchen stuff so we're ready to eat soon? Dewey, your room's the first door down the hall."

Then excited again, Dewey kicked off his sneakers and headed down the hall to his room, where his excitement faded as quickly as it came when he saw its size.

It took less than two hours to unpack and place each item in its permanent or temporary spot, and after Avriel and Lisa had finished putting together the two beds, Avriel insisted on picking up Chinese food for supper, the Chinese food that Lisa had introduced him to and had since become their celebratory meal.

With Avriel and Dewey having gone to pick up the food, Lisa flattened the many empty cardboard boxes, stacked them on the kitchen table, and used a kitchen chair to keep the apartment's door open. Determined to take it all in one trip, she scooped up the stack of cardboard that almost reached the top of her head, leaned her body back so the flattened boxes rested against the side of her turned head, and carefully navigated through the apartment's entrance and down the hall where she walked forward while keeping her head turned toward the wall on the right, which she noticed could use a fresh coat of paint. When she stopped at the door to the garbage room on her right and lifted a leg to push open its knobless door, most of the cardboard slid forward and dropped to the floor.

Lisa's frustration turned to surprise when she saw a tall,

good-looking man a few years older than her standing in front of her. Suddenly shy, she looked down at the cardboard by their feet and noticed his tight jeans accentuating his firm thighs, and as she looked up, noticed his muscular chest standing out in a tight solid-blue T-shirt where under one sleeve was a cigarette package being crushed under the strain of the material. Her eyes followed the man's muscular neck up to his clean-shaven face still bronzed from the summer before and sporting a chiseled jaw, a thin straight nose, and brown eyes. With his smile revealing a set of almost perfectly aligned but not exactly white teeth, his wavy brown hair hanging just past his ears seemed to request respect. Blushing, she stammered, "S-sorry. I-I didn't see you in front of me."

"I didn't think you could see anything in front of you," he joked, revealing a slight French accent as he bent down to stack the cardboard resting at their feet.

"Thanks, but... but I can do that."

"It's not a problem. Just being neighborly."

Using both arms to carry the cardboard, he used his foot to push open the garbage room's door, and while almost entranced by his tightly-jeaned butt, she followed him in with the rest of the cardboard and became even more entranced when he bent over and made a neat pile in the back corner of the room. Then with the noxious smell of the room snapping her mind back, she placed her cardboard on top of his pile and the two left as the door closed behind them, trapping most of the smell inside.

Stiffly holding out her hand, she said, "Well... thanks. I'm... I'm Lisa. I just moved down the hall with my son, Dewey."

Taking her hand, the man held it instead of shaking it and said, "Hi Lisa. I'm François, but most call me Frank. I'm in apartment two," and then instead of shaking it, he lifted her hand slightly while bending down to kiss the back of it.

Catching him looking her up and down, she quickly pulled her hand back before his lips touched it. "Well... I have to... to get back. Thank you... thanks again for your help, François."

Nervously turning back toward her apartment, she could feel her neighbor's eyes on her and found herself having to think about how to walk as she made the short trip back.

"Welcome to the building, Lisa," François called out.

Lisa looked back and waved before entering her apartment, where she moved the chair away from the door, and after it closed, leaned up against it to calm her pounding heart.

To Lisa, François was a very good-looking man, but he seemed a bit overconfident, which took away from his looks. His apparent interest in her flattered her, but it also made her guarded. He excited her and he scared her, or maybe she scared herself. Then she thought of Ruth, who she was sure would've liked him. François and his pretentious attempt to kiss her hand would've amused the old woman.

Taking a deep breath, she exhaled, "Françoooooois," and released her first laugh in two weeks.

CHAPTER 5
Blue and Stevie

The next day, Saturday, the sun failed to follow its ten-year morning protocol. It didn't wake Dewey. It couldn't. It came up on a different side of the building, and even if it came up on his side, the pickup parked just outside his bedroom window would've blocked most of its morning rays.

An hour later than usual, Dewey woke, and still half asleep, sat up and looked around his room, confused. It was as if someone, maybe Avriel, had snuck in while he slept and quietly rearranged everything, including the walls. The only thing that remained in its proper place was the window, which was larger than it should've been. To the right of the door, where there should've been five feet of wall with his small desk pushed up against it, there were, instead, the double sliding doors of a closet that was narrower than it should've been, and his desk was on the left side of his bed. His toy box, dresser, and one nightstand were against the opposite wall with only a foot of space between them and the foot of the bed, and instead of white walls with posters stapled to them, the bare walls were painted in an ugly shade of yellow with a lighter shade of squares and rectangles scattered about, which he assumed were where pictures had once hung. It took Dewey a few seconds to remember it was his new room and another second to decide he didn't like it.

Adding to his dislike, when he got out of bed, he noticed the front bumper of the pickup on the other side of his window. Closing his curtains, he wouldn't open them again for some time.

Dewey pulled up his purple pajama bottoms and headed down the hall and into the narrow kitchen, where his nostrils were filled with the noxious fumes of the cleaner his mother was using to scrub the light-gray industrial vinyl tiles covering its floor.

Lisa heard her son's footsteps approaching and without looking up, said, "Hi, Honey. Please wash your face and brush your teeth. When I'm done here, I'll make you breakfast, maybe in ten minutes."

Dewey said nothing as he turned around and walked down the hall to the small bathroom at its end, deciding he didn't like the apartment any more than he did his bedroom.

In his coveralls from the day before, Avriel showed up a few minutes later carrying two paintbrushes, a paint roller attached to a long pole, and several old bedsheets. He had smelled the cleaner as he walked down the building's hallway and thought it was an improvement over the odor from the day before, but when he entered the apartment and got its full impact, causing him to think it might've burned some of his nose hairs, he offered to take his friends to breakfast at what had become their favorite diner, which was near the Armdale Rotary, the entrance to Herring Cove Road.

Lisa was more than happy to agree, and as they were leaving, she considered opening the windows to get rid of the smell, but then it crossed her mind that someone could easily break in.

The breakfast was the highlight of Dewey's morning. He liked the selection of bread for the toast, the choice of how he liked his eggs, the two pancakes, the bacon, the fresh fruit, and his choice of juice along with the small glass of milk, but he didn't like the conversation between his mother and Avriel, so he ate in silence as they discussed where they would start painting, who would paint what, and how much they planned to finish that day.

After arriving home and while Avriel and Lisa crammed themselves into the kitchen to paint it, Dewey played in his room with his G.I. Joes.

A couple of hours after lunch, when he became bored with his action figures, Dewey asked his mom if he could take his bike for its first-ever ride and she agreed on the condition that he dress warm, wear his mittens, and stay close to the apartment, which surprised him since he had asked only for the sake of asking. Two weeks earlier, he had asked the same thing, and she refused because of the chilly weather, the same chilly weather as that afternoon.

Avriel was as excited as his little friend, and he was going to offer to help him carry out the bike, but Lisa, knowing Avriel as she did, motioned for him not to. Her son would have to learn to do it on his own.

Dewey was more than happy to go through the struggle of getting his new ten-speed bike out of the building. With a facecloth he had borrowed from the bathroom, he wiped the months of dust from its frame, wheels, handlebars, pedals, and, to his mother's later alarm, its greasy chain before walking it down the hallway, struggling with its heavy frame up the metal stairs, where he made room for a mumbling man who struggled not to stumble down them, and navigating it through the lobby's interior and exterior glass doors.

Sitting on his bike where the gravel road met the building's asphalt parking lot and easily using the ball of his foot to stay upright, Dewey noticed the feel of his new bike was very different from his old one, which he had named Flamer and which a truck had crushed the summer before last. Flamer's banana seat was more comfortable than his new bike's much smaller seat, and he could almost sit straight up on it, whereas on his new one, he had to lean forward, and even more so if he held onto where the black plastic-wrapped handlebars twisted into a half-loop on each side.

Pushing off the road with one foot, he pushed down on a pedal with the other and began riding in large circles. He wanted to go straight, but because he leaned slightly to one side, the bike wanted to go in that direction. It took a few minutes, but when he was able to center his body, he began riding up and down the gravel road, testing the front and back brakes one at a time before testing them together. Each time he squeezed a brake, the bike would slide on the gravel road, creating a small cloud of dust and a mild flashback to his bike accident the previous summer, the accident that had formally introduced him to Avriel's black Cadillac, to Avriel, and later that same evening, to Mrs. Rosen. The same accident that had sent him to the hospital with a fractured arm, a displaced shoulder, and several scrapes and cuts, with one needing stitches. That was the first and last time Dewey rode a ten-speed bike, and it was only for about thirty seconds.

Dewey thought he had better learn the gear system and began adjusting the two gear levers at the base of the handlebars to see their effect. Watching the chain switch between the two different-sized sprockets at the pedals and then looking back to watch it switch between the five progressively larger sprockets on the rear wheel, he soon figured out how much to move the levers to switch them in their proper order, and after a few minutes, he decided it was less work to keep the chain on the larger sprocket at the pedals and only adjust the lever for the sprockets on the rear wheel, using it as a five-speed bike instead of a ten.

Avriel would've liked to have been there for the bike's maiden voyage, but he had to make do with witnessing it from a distance. For the first few minutes of Dewey's bike riding, he and Lisa took a break from painting to watch him from the living room window, trying to spot him around the Cadillac blocking much of their view. They gasped when it appeared he was going to lose control and fall over, laughed when he regained control, and went back to painting when he could easily ride up and down the gravel road.

After half an hour of repeatedly riding up and down the road, a then confident Dewey stopped at the entrance of the street and watched the cars on Herring Cove Road fly past Autumn Drive.

Then wanting to explore the neighborhood, he pondered the condition his mother had given him. How far away would she consider not close to the apartment? Was it a physical distance or a time distance? Would biking as far as the store, just two blocks to the right and on his side of Herring Cove Road, be too far? By foot, he was sure it was too far, but by bike, it could be less than five minutes there and back, possibly making it close enough to the apartment. Then deciding it was more a time distance rather than a physical distance, he pedaled up onto the sidewalk and headed toward the corner store.

It was only after the first car flew past him that he realized the potential danger so close to him. Each time he heard a car coming up from behind, he stopped pedaling, stiffened his small body, and tightened his grip on the handlebars, and as it passed, he relaxed and pedaled on.

Even with his sporadic pedaling, it only took seconds to reach the next street, where he decided to get off his bike and walk it past the two boys almost thirty feet away and taking up most of the sidewalk as they headed toward him. A little taller than him, they looked like twins with their matching spring jackets and their extreme amount of freckles. Strangely, one boy carried a long wooden pole from what could've once been a broom.

The first boy, the empty-handed one, said loudly to the other, "Hey, isn't dat yer bike there?"

The boy carrying the pole replied, "Yeah! Hey, kid! Me thinks dat's my bike ya stealed there!"

With Dewey's curiosity with the boys replaced by confusion and then fear, he stopped walking his bike and was considering turning around and going back home when they ran up to him.

"I said dat's 'is bike. Now gives it 'ere!" demanded the first boy.

"No, it's not... and I won't!" Dewey forced out before instinctively turning the bike sideways, creating a barrier between him and the boys.

The second boy said, "We'll sees aboots that, eh?" and wound up to swing the pole.

Picking the bike up, Dewey stepped back and used it to block the pole that clanged against the bike's frame. Then with a courage that seemed to come naturally, he stepped forward with it, and with the pole bouncing off its frame a second time, the pole-wielding boy quickly stepped backward and poked the pole into his partner, who stepped back, cursed, tripped, and fell on his back.

"Hey! Earl, Graham! What the hell are yas doin'?" someone shouted from behind Dewey.

As the eyes of both boys widened, Dewey became even more afraid. Whoever could frighten those two boys so quickly would have to be worse than them!

With the boy holding the pole standing frozen, the other got himself to his feet and yelled, "This kid stole Graham's bike and we're tryin' ta get it back!"

"Pigshit!" said a taller redheaded boy appearing on Dewey's right. "This is Dewey 'ere's bike, and Dewey's my friend, and if yas gotta problem with 'im, yas gotta problem with me!"

Mumbling that they had no problem, the two boys crossed the road and walked back toward the steep street that, from Dewey's angle, appeared to peek out from the forest.

"Thanks," Dewey said, relieved that the boys were gone and the person who had put the fear into them, and him, was the boy he met the day before.

"No problem. That's are welcomin' committee," Blue joked with a grin. "Ya handled yerself good there. Ya standed yer ground. Good for ya. Some kids would'a given 'em the bike and others would'a cried and yelled for help, but not ya. Ya got some balls, bud," he said, patting Dewey on the shoulder. "Where ya goin'?"

"Home now... I guess."

"Cool. I'll walk with ya... but hows abouts we walk ta the store first? It's just at the corner up there and just takes a minute."

Trying to appear as if the recent event didn't bother him while not understanding what Blue meant by him having *some balls,* Dewey nodded his head and said, "Okay."

After Blue took the bike from Dewey, who was apprehensive about handing it over, he started walking it along between them, and noticing his bare hands, Dewey discreetly removed his mittens and shoved them in his jacket pockets.

"I saw ya there on yer bike at the end of Autumn Drive, but before I caughts up ta ya, ya was gone up Herring Cove Road. It's a nice bike ya gots 'ere. New?"

"Yup, my best buddy gave it to me for my birthday."

"Best buddy? The old guy?"

"Yup. He's Av... Avriel."

"Cool. So, yer eight?"

"Ten," Dewey replied, trying not to be insulted. "A small ten."

"Yeah, yer small, and so's Stevie."

"How old are you?"

"Twelve," he said as he moved his hand from the bare metal at the center of the handlebars to the black rubber-wrapped portion. "Stevie's yer age. The triplets back there are thirteen... just short fer their age too. Lucky for us, ya only met two of 'em. The third's the real *instagater*."

"How do you know which is which?" Dewey asked, then proud of himself for standing up to two thirteen-year-olds.

"The third triplet doesn't look the same. So, yer in five?"

"Yup. You?"

"Seven. Hey, I never saws ya at my school. Where ya comin' from?"

"Home."

"Right," Blue smiled. "I mean, where'd ya move from? What part of the city?"

"Gilmore Street."

"Yeah, I know Gilmore. It's across from Cowie Hill, right?"

"Yup. I saw you there once, running with Robby... Robby O'Brien."

"Huh? Oh, right, last summer. Yeah... no, we weren't runnin' with 'im. We were runnin' after 'im. I didn't know 'is name. Stevie and me saw 'im by Frank's friend's place teasin' his retarded daughter." Blue stopped walking the bike. "Hey! Now I remember ya! Yer the kid with the crushed glider and the cast on his arm, right?"

"Right! That was me!" Dewey said, flattered to be remembered, and then before he could ask who Frank was, Blue asked if he got the cast from a fight. "No. I-I got in a car accident," Dewey said, finding the boy's question strange. "Did you... did you fight with Robby... after you caught up with him? Did you... was it you who gave him the black eyes? He had them the next day after I saw you running with... after him."

"Nah, that was Stevie," Blue said, walking Dewey's bike again. "This place is likes a different world ta ya, huh?"

"I guess. Is it always like this? Are there more like the twins... the triplets?"

"No, and yes. It can be worse. Likes I said, those were only two of 'em. They live in the pubs up there."

"The pubs?" Dewey asked as they crossed the street to the corner store.

"Public housing, back there up Carson Street. There's dozens of houses at the top... townhouses owned by the city." With Dewey looking back toward the steep street, Blue added, "Ya can't see 'em. They're at the top. Frank says it's the city's way a tryin' ta hide all the poor people. It's called Rockin' Stone Heights 'cause of a giant rock that rocks back and forth... or used ta. People tried ta crush so much shit under it, it hardly moves now," Blue said and then gestured for Dewey to open the store's glass door so he could wheel in the bike.

Inside, Blue waved to a short and heavy balding man behind the counter. "Hey, Mr. Delaney."

"Hey, Blue! How's it goin' and how's the old man?"

"I'm good, and he's still movin' and shakin'," Blue said as he leaned the bike up against the counter and headed to the back of the store, with Dewey following. Stopping at the shelves of the smaller bags of potato chips, he began examining their corners, and after a minute, said, "Cool! I found one!" and showed the bag of chips to Dewey. "Hey, try ta find more bags with this thin red line inside its folded corner 'ere."

Holding himself back from asking why, Dewey nodded his head before searching the bags on the two lower racks while Blue continued searching through the three top ones, and by the time they finished, each had found another bag with a thin red line inside its pleated corner.

On the way to the front of the store, Blue grabbed a pint of orange juice, placed it and the bags of chips on the counter, and handed two empty chip bags and a two-dollar bill to Mr. Delaney, who looked inside the empty foil bags and said, "Two more free ones? Blue, you've the luck of the Irish."

Blue smiled mischievously. "Ya know how it is, but don't tell Frank. He'd hate ta know I got somethin' from my mother."

"Right. Hey, who's your quiet friend there? A cousin of Stevie?"

"No, he's new 'ere."

Dewey held out his hand. "Hi. I'm Dewey. I live in the same building as Blue."

Reaching across the counter, Mr. Delany smiled and shook the boy's hand. "Well, young man, ya have as good a tour guide as any. Take care and I hope you enjoy your stay here in this *fine* neighborhood," he said before placing the items in a white plastic bag and handing it and the change to Blue, who offered the bag to Dewey.

Taking the bag, Dewey said, "Thank you, sir," and followed Blue as he wheeled the bike out of the store.

"You're welcome, young man. Every polite gentleman is welcome here. We don't get enough of them. Blue, don't be corrupting him," Mr. Delaney laughed.

"I will," Blue replied as the door closed. "Hey, Art, what's happenin'?"

"Short cigs," the lean man said as he stopped at the entrance to the store. "And ya?"

"Just hangin'."

"Cool. Hey, ya up fer some huntin' tomorrow?"

"Can't tomorrow. I'm doin' a movie."

"Next time, then. Hey, new bike?"

"Nope, it's Dewey's 'ere. He just moved inta are buildin', apartment eight."

"Nice meetin' ya, Dewey."

Shaking away his fascination with how the man's long dark hair hanging down the sides of his head seemed to blend into his mustache curving down the sides of his chin, Dewey said, "Uh... you too, sir," he said, embarrassed for being caught staring.

"Later, guys," Art said as he entered the store, leaving the boys to walk back the way they came.

"You hunt?" Dewey asked.

"Not really. I go with 'im while 'e practices with 'is bow. I use 'is pellet gun ta shoots squirrels and things. Art's a crack shot. He can hit a small bird with just an arrow. And 'e's... he's... uh... different. He can't remember nothin'. It takes 'im forever to remember names and things ya tells 'im, so don't be surprised if 'e asks ya yer name a few times," Blue said, changing sides with Dewey so he could wheel the bike along the dirt shoulder of the sidewalk. "Ya'll see 'im on the steps of are buildin' carvin' away. He's pretty good at it. He carves things like dragons, birds, and stuff. I think 'e sells 'em or somethin', 'cause 'e carves a lot." Then walking in silence for a minute, Blue asked, "Ya was born with the name?"

"No, it's really Dwight, but Mommy and Daddy called me it, and now everyone does."

Blue stopped. "Mommy? Daddy? Really? Okay, ya have

ta stops that. No one 'round 'ere uses *mommy* and *daddy*. It's... it's mom and dad... and ya know what? It's goin' ta have ta be Dwight too. Dewey sounds way too wimpy, and it's goin' ta get ya in more fights than ya wants... esp'cially if ya says *mommy* and *daddy*," Blue said before pausing for a second to stare at a blushing Dewey. "So, who calls ya Dewey?"

"Mommy... mom," Dewey said with his face reddening more.

"Right," Blue grinned.

Continuing their walk, they crossed the next street and two minutes later turned left onto Autumn Drive where Dewey, trying not to appear hopeful that they might hang out together, asked, "What... what are you doing after this?"

"Meetin' up with Stevie in twenty."

"Oh," Dewey said, trying to hide his disappointment.

"Ya wanna come?"

At that moment, if Dewey was to rate his joy from the lowest being one to the highest being ten, it was most definitely a ten.

"Sure! Uh... yeah, I can do that, but... but I'll have to drop my bike off at home first," he said, trying hard to hide the excitement that could make him look like a little kid.

"Okay, I'll comes with ya. I have ta get some stuff from home, so we'll drop this off at yer place and then head ta mine."

Dewey held the building's front door open for his new friend, who with one arm balanced the bike in the air by its frame as he walked up the cement steps and into the lobby where he used his key to open the inside door. As he continued to carry the bike, they made their way down the stairs and through the smells and noises of the hallway. At Dewey's apartment door, Blue set the bike on the floor and put a hand on Dewey's shoulder, stopping him from opening it. "Hey, what's yer last name?"

"Dixon."

"Cool," Blue said, relieving Dewey of the plastic bag and gesturing for him to open the door.

Inside, Dewey took his bike from Blue and leaned it against the unpainted wall to the left of the door. "Mommy... Mom, Av, I'm back."

Blue followed Dewey into the living/dining room where on the floor were old bedsheets acting as drop cloths and two opened cans of paint resting on flattened-out garbage bags with a small puddle of white paint surrounding one can. Avriel, in his coveralls, was painting into the corners while Lisa, in a T-shirt and old jeans, was rolling the paint onto the wall, and when both turned to Dewey, they were surprised to see him with somebody. "Hi, Honey. Who's your friend?"

"Mom, this is Blue. He lives in the building. Av and I met him yesterday."

"It's nice to meet you again, sir, and nice to meet you, Mrs. Dixon."

"Same here, young man," Avriel said.

"Hi, Blue," Lisa said. "Which apartment are you in?"

"Apartment two at the other end of the hall. You two are doing a great job."

"Thanks, but it'll take at least another coat. Apartment two? You're... you're François' son?"

"That's right," Blue nodded his head.

"It's a small building. I met him yesterday."

Dewey cut in. "Mom, Blue saved me from some guys who wanted to take my bike."

"Take your bike?"

"It was nothing, Mrs. Dixon," Blue answered for Dewey. "Some kids who never saw Dwight before thought they would bother him. I just had to let them know I knew him and all was *copathetic* after that."

A semi-shocked Lisa said, "Oh, okay... well... well, thank you, Blue."

"Mom, can I go hang out with him, please?" Dewey asked with pleading eyes.

Surprised by the question, since it seemed so foreign coming from her son, Lisa paused a second. "Uh... sure... sure, you can. Just don't go far. We're having supper at five. Blue, you're welcome to join us if you'd like."

"That sounds great. I'd like that," Blue said, surprising Dewey with his quick acceptance without first finding out what they were having. "If it's okay with you, Mrs. Dixon, I'd like to give Dwight a tour of the neighborhood."

"Sure, since you strike me as a responsible gentleman," Lisa said with a smile, "And we'll see you both at supper, around five?"

"For sure. It's nice meeting you, Mrs. Dixon, and, sir," Blue said before leaving the apartment.

"Bye, Mom. Bye, Av," Dewey said as he closed the door behind him.

With Lisa and Avriel returned to painting, neither commented on it, but they were glad Dewey had made a friend.

Then, with it just occurring to her, Lisa asked, "Av, did you notice Dewey called me mom, not mommy?"

As the two walked toward Blue's apartment, Dewey said, "You talked differently around my mom," and then wished he hadn't said it. Perhaps Blue didn't realize it. Perhaps he was pointing out a fault and offending his new friend.

"Yeah, there's a way ta talks ta kids 'ere and a way ta talks ta adults. Remember, I striked yer mom as a gentleman. Ya always has ta talk proper ta adults ya just met, so they respects ya." Then Blue answered Dewey's next question before he could ask it. "I could talks like that all the time, but it takes effort, like tryin' ta speak in that old man's accent all the time. It's easier talkin'... talkin' lazy, and if I didn't, if I talked like that all the time, kids 'round 'ere would stop givin' me respect."

"Respect?"

"Yeah. Ya needs it 'ere or ya got nothin'. Those triplets left ya alones 'cause they respects me."

"They looked afraid of you."

"Afraid, respect, same thing if they does whats ya wants. Hey, the old man and yer mom got somethin' goin' on?"

"Huh?"

"Boyfriend and girlfriend?"

"Ew! No, nothing like that, just best buddies!"

Blue laughed. "Cool. He's married?"

Recovering from the boyfriend and girlfriend question, Dewey said, "He was, but his wife died last summer."

At his apartment door, Blue put his ear against it and stood there for a few seconds, listening. Then smiling, he winked at Dewey and quickly opened it, just missing one man and hitting a thinner one who had been standing on one foot trying to squeeze the other into a tied sneaker. The man cursed as he fell into the narrow kitchen, landing on his back with both hands still holding onto his half-on sneaker. Cursing again, he squeezed his foot into the sneaker and stood up to reveal his average height and long hair, which to Dewey would have made him look like a woman if not for his few days of facial growth and the black tattoo of a serpent on his forearm. Tucking in his solid-black T-shirt and adjusting the cigarette pack stuffed under its sleeve, the man growled, "Damn, Blue! Ya gotta starts wearin' a bell around yer neck! Frank, get 'im a bell will ya!"

Blue smirked. "Sorry, Tim. Never saw ya there. Frank, this 'ere's Dwight Dixon from Apartment eight. He just moved in yesterday."

"Hi, Dwight," the other man said, holding out his hand to shake. "I'm Blue's dad." And shaking the boy's hand, he asked, "Apartment eight? Lisa's son?"

"Yes, sir," Dewey answered, trying to place Frank's accent that wasn't British like Avriel's, and then following Blue's earlier example and finding it interesting that their apartment had the same layout as his, but in the opposite direction, he added, "And it's a nice place you have here, sir."

Tim cut in, "Dwight, hold back that opinion until ya see Frank's whole place. Ya mights just have ta adjust it. Hey, yer a Dixon, eh?"

"Yes, sir."

"Ya related ta Gary Dixon?"

"No, I don't think so."

"Ralph Dixon?"

"No, sir."

"Tom?"

"No, sir."

"Dick?"

"No."

"Harry?"

"No."

"Paul?"

"Paul? Yeah! He's my dad! You knew my dad?"

"Nope."

"But you know a Paul Dixon?"

"Nope."

"But you said Paul Dixon."

"Well, really, I just said Paul, but I don't know 'im. Gotta go, but it was fun, Dwight."

After Tim picked up a paper lunch bag from off the floor and left the apartment, Frank closed the door. "Dwight, next time just ignore him."

"Yeah, he's touched in the head," Blue added.

Then hearing Tim greet someone as he headed down the hall toward the back door of the building, Blue gestured for Dewey to listen.

"Hey, Mrs. Publicover, Mary saids ta say hi ta ya."

"Mary? Do you mean Mary McNeal?" asked a voice of an older woman.

"Nope, Mary Gordon."

"I don't think I know a Mary Gordon, Timothy."

"Funny, that's just what she says too."

"Timothy Williams, you're a very strange boy!"

"I gets that a lot. Have a good day, Mrs. Publicover."

"It can only go up from here, Timothy!"

Blue tapped his head. "Touched. But what do ya expect from a grown man who lives with 'is mom?"

"Come on, Blue. He's only been back a little while now."

"Frank, it's been over a year."

"That long? Wow, time flies. Hey, are you guys staying?"

"Nah, I have ta grab some stuff and then we're goin' ta meets up with Stevie," Blue said before he went into the small kitchen, opened the fridge door that blocked the kitchen's entrance, and bent down behind it.

"So, Dwight, are... are your folks divorced?" Frank asked.

"Huh?"

"Are they living apart?"

"No... well, they were... but he died."

"Oh, I'm sorry to hear that. How'd he go... if it's okay asking?"

"He fell down and hurt his neck."

"It sounds like it was a quick one, but if you have to go, go quick."

Blue stood up and closed the fridge door. "Frank, his mom's really pretty. He'll have another dad in no time."

Noticing the shock on Dewey's face, Frank said, "Now, Blue—"

"It's the truth. Hey, Dwight's mom invited me ta eats with 'em, so I'll see ya tomorrow mornin'," Blue told his father and then gestured for Dewey to follow him as he left the apartment.

"Okay, à demain matin," Frank said, enlightening Dewey to his accent. "Dwight, it was nice meeting you."

"You too, sir," Dewey said, looking back as Frank closed the door.

With Blue leading the way up the stairs, Dewey noticed the additional contents of the plastic bag were causing it to stretch. He would've asked what else he had in the bag, but his mind was on Blue's comment. He didn't want to believe his new friend was correct. He didn't want a new dad, a replacement dad, and then needing to get his mind off the comment, he asked, "Your dad's French?"

"Yeah."

"You speak French?"

"Not much."

Leaving the building to walk up the road, Dewey asked, "Is your mother working today?"

"No, she left us."

"She died?"

"I wish. No, she took off on us a few years ago."

Dewey was confused until it hit him that if a man could leave his wife and his child, as his father did before his accident, then why not a mother, though he couldn't imagine his mother leaving him.

Reaching Herring Cove Road, Blue looked both ways

before darting to the road's gravel shoulder on the other side.

Surprised, Dewey shouted to Blue, "I can't cross this road. I'm not allowed."

"What? Are ya serious? What are ya five? Come on! Who's ta know?" Blue shouted back.

Deciding he wouldn't let a road stand between him and a new friendship, Dewey let two cars pass before running across it, stopping for a moment at the dividing line before running the rest of the way.

When Blue jumped across the ditch and entered the woods, Dewey followed. With his free hand, Blue grabbed onto a branch and started making his way up a steep path. To Dewey, the path seemed to have suddenly shown itself, and following Blue, he grabbed at a branch with both hands and tried to keep up with his new friend as they climbed up the path for almost half a minute before it leveled out. After another minute, Blue turned left off the path and entered the woods, where the two maneuvered through the trees to come to a clearing surrounded by a twenty-foot square two-foot-high wall of rough stones. Inside the wall were several thin, rectangular slabs of rock, one sticking straight out of the ground, a few sticking up at odd angles, and the others resting flat. Sitting inside the square on the far rock wall, Blue laid the clinking plastic bag at his feet, and when Dewey sat next to him and a stone moved under his weight, he moved a few inches away from his new friend. "This is one of the places we hangs out at, but just on Saturdays."

Finding the place rather eerie and thinking he wouldn't want to be there alone, Dewey asked, "What is it? What's this place?"

"It's an old, old graveyard from the days of the first settlers. Ya can still read some of the writin' there on those stones, but just barely. A couple more minutes on the path and we'd be at Orange Walk, where Stevie lives... the first street off a Carson. He'll be 'ere in a minute. He's never late, and if 'e is, then there's a problem. Hey, speakin' of the Devil!"

Just as Stevie emerged from the trees, he stopped, looked at Dewey, and then with a question mark on his face, looked at Blue.

"He's cool... more than cool. He stood up ta the triplets all by 'imself."

Then with raised eyebrows and a couple of head nods, Stevie gave Dewey a thumbs-up and a flattered Dewey returned it.

"Well... two of them, anyway. Ian wasn't there."

Gesturing as if to say that made more sense, Stevie walked over and sat down on the other side of Blue, where he offended Dewey by whispering in Blue's ear.

"Yeah, gots everythin'," Blue said before leaning down to pick up the plastic bag and handing Dewey and Stevie each a bag of chips, keeping the last bag for himself. "I hope you like Salt and Vinegar, Dwight."

"Sure," Dewey said and went along with the two by opening his bag and silently eating the chips. After a few seconds, he noticed some printing on the inside of the bag and shook the chips around to read it. "Hey! I won a free bag of chips! Well... I guess, Blue, you won a free bag of chips. You paid for them," he said, and then with Blue and Stevie grinning at each other, he asked, "What?"

"It's yers. We always win 'em. That's why I tolds ya ta look for the red line. Stevie 'ere figured out the secret markin' for the winnin' bags."

"Seriously? That's genius!"

"Yeah, and thanks ta Stevie, we pretty much eats 'em for free. Keep the bag with ya fer the next time we go and gets some more."

"Sure, okay. That's really, really cool!"

When the boys had finished eating their potato chips, all wiped their greasy fingers on their jeans and Stevie handed his bag to Blue, who neatly folded up the two and placed them in the pocket of his jeans.

As Dewey folded up his empty bag, Stevie whispered to Blue, who grinned and said, "Hey, Dwight, just ta make sure ya know, this bag thing's a secret, eh? We don't wants everyone knowin' and takin' all the free chips... so if ya tells anyone, I'll have ta sic Stevie on ya."

Forcing a smile, Dewey nodded, said, "I won't," and received another thumbs-up from Stevie.

Picking up the plastic bag again, Blue pulled out three brown stubby glass bottles and handed one each to Stevie and Dewey, who noticed the label said Schooner Beer. Dropping the plastic bag containing only the orange juice to the ground, he pulled out three cigarettes from his jacket pocket and handed one to Stevie and one to a then apprehensive Dewey, who had to fight the urge to make up an excuse to go home.

Even though he knew both would get him into trouble with his mom, Dewey's growing curiosity about the beer and the cigarette soon outweighed his apprehension, and trying to be cool, he asked, "You guys do this all the time?"

"Nah, only on Saturdays," Blue answered as he handed a bottle opener to Dewey. "Ya like beer and smokes?"

"Sure," he lied. "I used to drink beer and smoke cigarettes with my dad... sometimes."

"Bullshit!" Stevie exclaimed, surprising Dewey with his high-pitched voice.

Ignoring Stevie, Blue asked, "Really?"

"No. Stevie's right. I never tried either of them," Dewey admitted with shame.

When Stevie gestured to Blue as if to say he had told him

so, Blue ignored him again and said, "That's cool. I was just a little younger than ya when I tried 'em. Open the beer and give 'er a try."

Then with Stevie leaning forward past Blue, the two watched as Dewey laid the cigarette down on the wall and nervously opened the beer, trying several times before succeeding. Putting the bottle to his lips, he took a gulp and began coughing, making his new friends smile.

"The first taste is always the worstest. It gets easier each time ya drinks it. Frank says it's an acquired taste, and it must be easy ta acquire 'cause everyone drinks it."

To demonstrate, Blue took the opener from Dewey, opened his bottle with ease, and took a large gulp, and after handing the opener to Stevie, the three began drinking.

For Dewey, the taste of beer didn't get any better with each sip, and he was put at ease a bit when he noticed Stevie slightly wincing when he took his first few gulps. Then feeling he had passed his first *cool* test and guessing the cigarette lying on the wall beside him was his second, he picked it up and asked for a light.

The surprise on Blue and Stevie's faces was noticeable, and without a word, Blue pulled a plastic lighter from his pocket and handed it to Dewey who took it, flicked it just as he had seen people do, and lit the cigarette on the first try. Sucking the smoke into his mouth, he held it there for a moment before releasing it slowly, finding it much easier than expected.

"Dwight, yer just suckin' it inta yer mouth. Ya gotta inhale 'er inta yer lungs. Hold the smoke in yer mouth ta cool 'er down and then slowly inhale 'er inta yer lungs."

Still trying to look cool, Dewey took a long and what he thought was an impressive drag of the cigarette and held the smoke in his mouth for a count of five. Inhaling it into his lungs, he was hit by a dizziness that upset his stomach, and then coughing several times, he stood up, turned around, and to the high-pitched laughter of Stevie, vomited outside of the wall.

"Just take little puffs until ya gets 'er down," Blue said as he nudged Stevie to stop laughing.

Collecting himself, Dewey sat back down, and doing as Blue said, found it easier to handle with smaller puffs.

As each sipped their beer and smoked their cigarette, Blue told Dewey about their school. Blue and Stevie went to Rocking Stone Heights at the far end of Carson Street. It was a tough school and almost evenly divided between Blacks and Whites. Then Blue suggested it would be a good idea for Dewey to hang out with them at school, at least at the beginning, so he would fit in faster and avoid the initial bullying by the other kids. Flattered, Dewey agreed, especially after what he had experienced earlier that day, but he was certain his new school was along Herring Cove Road, not on Carson Street. Dewey didn't know the name, but from its location, Blue knew the school he was talking about, and surprised that Dewey would be attending Central Spryfield Elementary School further up Herring Cove Road, he told him that he must be good in school to go there while living closer to theirs. He also felt that school would be better for him since there would be fewer tough kids or problem kids (as his teachers commonly referred to them) going there.

With their cigarettes butted out and their beers almost finished, Dewey found himself feeling slightly loopy as he watched Stevie whisper in Blue's ear and then heard Blue whisper back, "Yeah, I know, but we'll be callin'im Dwight. It sounds tougher."

"Yeah, we should probably call you Steven too," Dewey said, with the alcohol relaxing him.

Stevie's blue eyes went cold. He put down his beer and stood up with his fists raised for a fight.

Pulling him back down, Blue said, "Stevie sounds like a wimpy name, but he fights like the Tasmanian devil. His fists move so fast, most don't have a chance against 'im. His reputation makes up for his name," and to prove his point, he told Stevie to show him.

Stevie stood up again, walked about five feet in front of the two, and turned to face them. Putting his fists up, he threw combinations of hooks, straight punches, jabs, and uppercuts and ended by spinning around and throwing a back fist, impressing Dewey so much that he clapped.

Smiling, Stevie sat back down and drank the last drop of his beer.

"Can you teach me that stuff?"

After Stevie whispered in Blue's ear, Blue said, "He says, 'Yeah, but don't expects ta learn that shit in one day.'"

Startled by Blue's cursing and made bolder by the beer, Dewey said, "You shouldn't swear."

"It's not me. It's Stevie. He said it. I'm just repeatin' what 'e said," Blue grinned.

"You shouldn't swear, Stevie."

Stevie shrugged his shoulders before bouncing up from the wall with his bottle in hand, turning around, and throwing it at a five-foot-tall boulder standing among the trees about twenty feet behind them, and with a loud smash, the bottle burst against it. Then Blue got up and threw his bottle at the boulder, and hitting its mark, it burst too. Excited by the smashing glass, Dewey stood up and threw his bottle, but missing the boulder, it bounced on the soft ground behind it until stopping at a tree. With Blue's low laugh mixing with Stevie's high-pitched one, Dewey joined in with his embarrassed laugh falling somewhere in between the two, and after they stopped laughing, they returned to the wall where Stevie sat next to Dewey to put him in a playful headlock while ruffling his hair.

"So where's the name Dwight from?"

"My mom named me after my grandfather," Dewey said, fixing his straight hair. "Where does Blue come from?"

"My dad. My mom named me Bartholomew after no one. They called me Bart until I was seven, but I kept gettin' inta trouble at school. Kids called me Bart the Fart, so Frank took the B, L, and E, W from my name and then changed the E, W ta U, E. Frank's the coolest dad. Most dads 'ere, like Stevie's, deserts their kids when they leave their wives... or girlfriends, but mine lives with me. That's rare around 'ere and he gets lots of respect for that. Okay, lets finish up. We has to get goin' soon," Blue said before pulling out the pint of orange juice from the bag, opening it, taking four large gulps, and handing it to Dewey. "It hides the smell of beer."

Feeling like he couldn't drink anymore, Dewey put the container to his lips and forced down two large gulps. Passing the container back to Blue, he handed it to Stevie, who emptied it and let out a long burp.

"Okay, it's almost time," Blue said as he looked at his watch.

With Stevie and a curious Dewey following, Blue stood up and headed back to the path where the three made their way down its steep end to Herring Cove Road. To Dewey, it seemed much easier going up than going down. Several times during his descent, he had to stop and hang onto a branch until his head stopped its slight spinning, and when he finally reached the road, the three jumped over the ditch, crossed the street, and headed down Autumn Drive, where they walked half of its length before turning toward a triplex on the left. Walking to the back of it, they climbed a short embankment and entered the rear parking lot of a three-story apartment building facing the next street over, where on the other side there was a small playground with several teeter-totters, a merry-go-round, and two sets of swings, one tall and one short. At the taller set of swings, they sat on its wooden seats with most of their orange paint worn off, and with Dewey sitting between his new friends, all began casually swinging.

"It won't be long now," Blue said.

"What won't be long?" Dewey asked.

"The Jehovah's Witness sisters."

"Oh," Dewey said, not knowing what a Jehovah's Witness was.

Then, after they swung silently for a few minutes, Blue said, "Here they come!"

Two young girls, maybe ten or eleven years old, were walking down the street from the direction of Herring Cove Road, both in identical yellow dresses and both with their long brown hair pinned up, and as they walked by the playground, talking and giggling while shooting glances at the three boys, Blue slid off his swing. "I have ta go a courtin'," he told them as he walked with some speed toward the girls.

Dewey was about to follow when Stevie leaned over, grabbed him, and gestured for him to stay, and doing as he was told, Dewey sat on his swing and watched Blue exchange a few words with the girls before the taller one pushed him down onto his bottom and both girls kicked him as he sat there taking it. Panicking, Dewey slid off his swing, but Stevie pulled him back again, and after a few seconds of fighting the desire to intervene, Dewey glanced over at Stevie whose smile took up most of his face as he watched the two Jehovah's Witnesses continue to assault his older friend.

When the girls stopped kicking him and ran off, Blue got to his feet, brushed himself off, and walked back to the swings, where, with a full smile, he said, "I knows she likes me! I'm sure of it now!"

"How do you know?" Dewey asked, certain he didn't see either girl showing Blue any affection.

"She didn't hits me as hard as 'er sister."

"Oh... okay," Dewey said, thinking if courting involved kicking, he wanted nothing to do with it.

"It's ten ta five," Blue said, looking at his watch. "Dwight, do ya thinks yer mom'll let Stevie stay fer supper too?"

"Yeah, I'm sure she would. But I don't know what she's making."

"That's cool. I'm sure whatever it is, it's good."

"Don't you want to know what we're eating before you come over? What if it's something gross, like cow tongue or something?"

"Nah, that's just rude. Ya never ask what they're eatin' when people invites ya fer supper. Besides, when people invites ya, they always makes somethin' good."

With Blue and Stevie following him, Dewey entered his apartment, and when he took off his shoes at the entrance, they did the same.

"Mom, we're back."

Lisa, who was in the kitchen straining spaghetti noodles, turned toward the three standing by the door and said, "Great. Oh... and I see you made another friend. Hi, other friend."

As Stevie waved, Dewey said, "This is Stevie. Stevie, this is my mom."

After Stevie whispered in Blue's ear, Blue grinned. "I ain't sayin' that. Uh... Mrs. Dixon, Stevie says you're much too pretty to be a mother. Oh... and he asks if he may stay for supper."

Lisa giggled. "Of course he may, especially after telling me I'm pretty."

"He'll need to call his mom if that's okay."

"Of course. There's a phone in the living room. Dewey, show him where it is, please."

In the living room, Av was picking up the lid of a paint can when Dewey asked, "Av, do you remember Stevie from yesterday?"

"Yes, I do. Hello, Stevie. How are you today?" he asked as he sealed up a can of paint by gently patting down the lid with a hammer.

"He's doing great, sir," Blue answered for his friend.

Watching Stevie pick up the receiver of the phone, dial, wait, and then whispered for a few seconds, Dewey was impressed. He had never made a phone call. He had answered several but never made one. His mother had once made him memorize their phone number, but he never had a reason to call it, especially not from home.

Avriel watched as Stevie placed the phone back on the receiver and walked over to whisper in Blue's ear. "He has to be home by seven-thirty, Mrs. Dixon."

"Me too," Avriel said. "I can drive you home on time."

Looking strangely at the old man, Stevie hesitated before nodding his head and giving a thumbs-up.

After Avriel returned the thumbs-up, he went to the entrance closet to get a metal folding chair, and as he placed it at the table, Lisa placed a large plastic bowl of noodles in the middle of the table, along with a smaller plastic bowl of sauce and a plate of buttered sliced bread. And as Avriel set five places with plates and cutlery, Dewey filled five glasses with milk.

With Stevie sitting beside Blue, Lisa placed noodles and sauce on everyone's plates and said, "Dig in."

After a minute, she asked, "So, boys, what grades are you in?"

Blue swallowed the pasta in his mouth. "Seven, Mrs. Dixon, and Stevie's in grade four, grade four Special Ed."

With Stevie elbowing Blue and scolding him with his eyes, Lisa asked, "Do you two like school?"

"Yes, we're nothing without an education."

Then, after eating in silence for several minutes, Lisa broke it, saying, "Blue, I guess we probably should've invited your father."

"No, he wouldn't be able to come. He has to work tonight."

"Oh, what's he do?"

"Security. He's in charge of security at the mall, the Spryfield Mall. He works nights, six to six. Usually, he works Monday to Friday, but one of the guys is sick, so he's filling in for him."

"Who watches you while he's at work?"

"Me... I do. I watch myself. In this part of the city, we grow up faster and become independent sooner," Blue said proudly.

After exchanging glances with Avriel, she asked, "Do you have all the emergency numbers if there's a problem?"

"Sure, I have Frank's work number."

"What about the police or fire department?"

"No. I mean, I know them, but I'm to... to call him and then if we need to, he'll call them," Blue said with his face hinting at his discomfort with the conversation. "He doesn't want me calling them for just any little thing... and we got two types of fire distinguishers, one for grease fires and one for regular ones."

"Well, if there's a problem, you can always come to me. After all, I'm just down the hall."

"Thanks, Mrs. Dixon. I'll do that," Blue said with a nod, if only to end the questions.

Lisa had asked Stevie a few questions too, like where he lived, how old he was, and how many brothers and sisters he had, and found Blue's constant answering for him strange, but not as strange as when Stevie would whisper in Blue's ear and then Blue would speak for him.

Stevie reminded Avriel of a puppet from a children's television show called Mr. Dressup that he had come across while searching for something to watch one morning, but he couldn't recall the name of the puppet, a dog who only spoke through another puppet. The dog would whisper into the ear of the other puppet, a young girl puppet, and she would repeat what the dog had said. It bothered Avriel that he couldn't remember the name. It bothered him whenever he failed to recall something, making him worry he was losing his memory. He was going to ask Dewey, but changed his mind so as not to embarrass anyone if they made the connection with the name. Then during their dessert of rice pudding, the name finally came to him and he surprised everyone by blurting out, "Finnegan!" Embarrassed, he told them that was what the British shouted after a splendid meal, and holding up his empty glass, he repeated, "Finnegan!" and the boys did the same.

Lisa found it strange that it was the first time she had heard of such a custom, and then the connection between Stevie and Finnegan hit her and she tried to hide her laugh by coughing into her paper napkin. When she got control of herself, she lightly kicked Avriel's shin, and he pretended not to notice.

Dewey went to bed in a much better mood than he had woken up with. He had made two friends on the very first day at his new place, and at that rate, he figured he would make hundreds in a year, but then he wondered what he would do with hundreds of friends. He wanted best buddies and a person could only have four, as Avriel had once told him he had read in a law book, making them rare and special, and having room for only one more after Blue and Stevie, he would carefully have to decide who that one would be among all the hundreds of friends he expected to make.

Besides making two new friends, Dewey was glad to have tried beer and cigarettes, but he enjoyed neither. He was also glad to have learned something about courting, but what he learned was more of a deterrent, and he was proud to have his first-ever secret, and that evening before going to bed, he had to fight off the strong urge to tell Avriel about his day and risk it slipping out. He didn't want to break the confidence of his new friends and maybe get two black eyes from Stevie, although he suspected Blue was just joking about siccing Stevie on him.

CHAPTER 6
Two Friends and a Movie

There was a soft tap on the apartment door. No one heard it, so no one answered it, so a few seconds later came a harder one.

Wearing what looked like the same painting clothes as the day before, Lisa opened the door to find their redheaded neighbor in only his tighty-whities.

"Good morning, Mrs. Dixon," Blue smiled.

"Hi, Blue. Come... come on in," Lisa grinned while moving out of the way for him to enter. "What's going on?" she asked, expecting there to be a minor problem.

"Not much. I want to see if Dwight would be up for seeing a movie with Stevie and me this afternoon. Freaky Friday's playing at the Spryfield Mall."

"He's seen that one, but I'm sure he'd like to see it again," Lisa said before turning her head toward the hallway and calling out, "Dewey, you have a visitor."

From inside his bedroom where old bedsheets covered most of his furniture, Dewey stopped painting around the baseboards to exchange surprised looks with Avriel, who paused from rolling white paint onto the ceiling and gave his little friend a thumbs-up.

"I'll be there in a minute," Dewey shouted and then looked around for the rags they were using to wipe the paint from their hands.

"Okay," Lisa called back. "It's Blue." And taking advantage of the delay, she whispered, "Blue, I already talked to Dewey about it, but has your father talked to you about talking to strangers?"

"Oh... sure," Blue whispered back while nodding his head and tilting down his eyebrows to exaggerate the seriousness of the topic. "With those two murders, I'm not to talk to strangers. I'm to keep walking if they approaches... approach me."

"That's good to hear it. I wasn't sure if you knew about those. I don't think Dewey knows about the second and I'd prefer he didn't, but he knows to avoid strangers. So, how are you getting to the mall? I'm sure Av would drive you."

"No, that's fine, Mrs. Dixon. Thanks for the offer, but we'll walk. Stevie and I walk there all the time."

"Is there a shortcut? Which way do you go?"

"There's really only one way to go. We take Herring Cove Road. It's thirty minutes at most. There's lots of traffic and all that, so there's no worry about strangers there," Blue said, hiding his frustration with the questions while removing Lisa's concern about them taking a secluded shortcut.

In his coveralls, with fresh white paint stains proudly added to a couple of old green ones, Dewey fought to hide his excitement as he met his new friend at the door and then fought to hide his surprise at finding him in only his underwear.

With the five-dollar bill his mother had given him stuffed into the back pocket of his jeans, his jacket opened and his mittens shoved in its pockets, just as Stevie and Blue were doing, a chilly but excited Dewey walked on the dirt shoulder of the sidewalk next to Blue, and as they passed the hill on their left lined with bungalows going to its top, Stevie, on the other side of Blue, whispered into Blue's ear, causing him to ask Dewey, "Ya been in a lot a fistfights?"

Startled by the question, Dewey answered, "No. No, never."

"Never? Not even one?"

"Never, ever, and I don't want to either," Dewey admitted.

"That's... that's cool. I just thought with the way ya handle the triplets, ya were at least in a few. They're really no biggy... no big deal. The first's always the worstest."

"You guys get in them often?" Dewey asked, becoming afraid of the answer.

"No, but they happen. The big trick ta avoid 'em is ta pretends ya don't cares. If ya keeps a brave face, it'll mess the other guy up, maybe even scare 'im off 'cause 'e don't knows what yer thinkin'. If ya looks scared, he'll thinks yer easy pickin's and try ta start one. Ya always has ta keep a brave face, a face like this. Look."

Blue stopped walking, and as his face lost all expression, he stared coldly at Dewey, who wasn't sure what to think. Was Blue angry with him or was that the expression he was talking about?

Then smiling, Blue said, "Scary, huh?"

"Yeah, I–I guess. You... you sort of look crazy," Dewey replied. "So, why would someone want to try to fight me?"

"To sees whats yer made of... and maybe for some braggin' rights," Blue said as they continued walking.

"Okay. So, I have to start practicing the brave face... in a mirror, I guess, right?"

"Yeah. It takes some work to get over the fear the first few times ya has someone in yer face, so ya has ta hides it at first. The trick I learned from Frank is ta sing a song in my head. Ya keep eye contact with the other guy, and makin' yer serious face, ya sings a song in yer head. It distracts yer mind and helps ya from bein' scared." Then Stevie whispered in his ear and he said, "Stevie says he'll teach ya ta fight. Ya has ta learn. Usually, ya gets in one and no one bothers ya again, win or lose. But if ya gets yer butt kicked, ya have ta do it like a man, no cryin'."

"Right, no crying," nodded Dewey, hoping for a change of topic since he was drowning in the stress of having to learn to make a brave face, learn to fight, and learn not to cry when he gets his butt kicked.

As the three walked in silence the rest of the way to the mall, Dewey found it odd that all the kids coming toward them had moved onto the dirt edge of the sidewalk and greeted Blue and Stevie with a 'Hey,' a nod of the head, or both. They all seemed to know the two. The first three times, Dewey moved out of their way to walk behind Blue and Stevie, but after the fourth time, he stayed behind them. It made it difficult to talk, but Dewey was okay with that.

Not wearing a watch, Dewey thought the trip took about thirty minutes, and with the anxiety brought on by their conversation, he couldn't wait to plop himself into a seat and lose himself in the movie.

It was Sunday. The mall was closed and the only way into the cinema was through its glass doors at the back of the building, where there was a smaller parking lot.

At the ticket counter, with Blue holding up three fingers, an old man in a wheelchair bumped him to the side. "Out of my way! One senior!" the man yelled as he placed a crinkled bill on the counter, and after grabbing his ticket and change from the noticeably uncomfortable ticket girl, he yelled, "Out of my way!" and rode over Blue's foot as he wheeled himself toward the concession counter.

"See that, guys?" Blue asked loud enough for most to hear, including the old man. "A jerk in a wheelchair is still a jerk!" Then, holding up three fingers again, Blue passed a twenty to the young woman.

Realizing he was paying for him too, Dewey protested, telling Blue his mother had given him money, but when Blue turned to him and used his scary glare, he consented.

"See! It works, right? Right?" Blue said, breaking a large smile.

"Right... I guess," Dewey said. "Thanks... thanks for buying my ticket."

"Now ya gets ta keep that money for somethin' else ya wants. Yer mom'll never know," Blue said as he picked up the tickets and change and handed Stevie and Dewey their tickets. "Okay, pop and popcorn are on me too, unless ya has a problem with that too, Dwight," he said, glaring again at Dewey, who shook his head. "I'm just messin' with ya, not abouts the pop and popcorn, but the face. Ya has ta remember that behinds it, I'm smilin'."

Five minutes later and with a giant pop and a carton of popcorn, which was larger than his head, Dewey sat with his friends, and after the lights had dimmed, all sat quietly watching the movie while occasionally laughing together.

Almost halfway through the movie, a boy returning from the washroom walked down the dark aisle, and as he got to their row, he stopped and stared at their partially lit faces. Then, after he had joined his group of friends further down and they whispered among themselves, they got up and sat in the seats behind Dewey and his new friends. A minute later, when Stevie, Blue, and Dewey turned to look back at the boys, Dewey recognized the two triplets from the day before, but this time, there was a third standing out from his brothers by several prominent scars on his chin and left cheek.

"Hey," Blue said, "Yas minds not kickin' are seats?"

The scarred one said, "Yeah, we mind. What ya goin's ta do aboots it?"

As Stevie went to stand, Blue grabbed him by his belt and pulled him back down. "Well, Ian, enjoy. If there's anythin' we can do ta help, just say it." Then looking at Dewey, he said, "Let's move."

With Dewey's hope of relaxing at the cinema gone, the three got up and walked to the back row of chairs, where they sat until the credits came up.

Putting their giant empty cups and empty cartons into the garbage cans lining the exit, the three headed to the concession counter, where Dewey nervously looked around, and not seeing the group of boys who had earlier bothered them, he relaxed.

After asking for a large cup of ice, Blue said to the two in a cold voice, "I gotta use the can."

With the washroom to themselves, the three chose their stalls, and after a few seconds, two toilets flushed, and Blue and Dewey came out and went to the line of sinks. Using the brown paper towel to dry their washed hands, Blue said over the sound of Stevie's stream, "Stevie has the bladder of a horse," which would've amused Dewey if not for Blue's continuing cold voice.

Without a flush, Stevie appeared from the stall, washed his hands, and as the three were leaving, he smiled and flicked the water from his wet hands at Dewey, causing him to smile too.

Following the last of the moviegoers through the exterior glass doors, the cool spring air hit them in the face, but that didn't stop Dewey from breaking into a sudden sweat when he saw the group of five boys waiting for them.

"Sorry to keep ya waiting," Blue said to them.

"No problem,. I hopes yas washed yer hands after yas

pissed," the scar-faced triplet said.

"No. We figures we'll wipe 'em clean with yas."

Dewey could hardly believe what was happening, and struggling to search for a song, he found a short one he knew all the words to and began singing it in his head.

"So that's the kid whose gots are bike, eh?" the third triplet asked his brothers, who nodded their heads. "My brother tells me ya stopped 'em from gettin' are bike back."

"Ya mean, I stopped them from stealin' 'is bike, and 'e didn't needs my help. He already had one on the ground before I even got there," Blue said. "Dwight here is tougher than 'e looks."

"Well, after today, yas won't stop 'em from doin' nothin'!"

"Yeah, we'll have ta see abouts that, Ian."

As Blue and Ian stood staring each other down, Dewey continued to sing the song in his head as he looked at Ian, whose face was expressionless and whose fists were clenched tightly by his sides, looked at Blue, whose hands were in his jacket pockets while he wore his scary face, and looked at Stevie, whose his fists were up while he was smiling. Looking at the expressionless faces of the other boys, the glimmer of a pocket knife's blade caught his attention, and he panicked. Struggling to restart the song he had sung once in his head, he had to search for the words, and when he found them again, he sang them aloud, "I'm a little teapot, short and stout!" Then lost in the flashback to when he had first sung the song in his grade one class recital, he placed his right arm on his hip, "Here is my handle," and stretched his other out to the side, "Here is my spout!"

With the group of five staring dumbly at the singing boy, Blue pulled two long cotton sacks from his jacket pockets, and swinging their heavy ends, he and Stevie charged at them.

"When I get all steamed up, hear me shout!"

It was as if the five boys had become mannequins. In the short period of Blue and Stevie's attack, not one of the five had time to get their fists up. With the blur of the swinging sacks mixing with the blur of Stevie's fist, all three triplets and one other boy had fallen to the ground. The last boy at the back had just enough time to get out of there.

"Tip me over and pour me out!"

As Dewey was tilting his body to the left side, Blue and Stevie returned to him.

"That was great!" Blue said, grinning at Dewey, who was then trying to force himself away from the song that was trapped in his head. "Ya distracted 'em longs enough for us ta cream 'em!"

With his brothers hobbling away, Ian got himself to his feet, and with a bloody nose and shaking hands, he struggled to pull the blade from a small pocketknife, and as he stepped toward the back of Stevie, Dewey screamed, "I'M A LITTLE TEAPOT SHORT AND STOUT!"

Both Blue and Stevie spun around and let loose a fury of strikes on Ian, causing the pocketknife to fly in the air and Ian to drop to the ground.

While the triplet groaned and tried to get to his feet, Blue reached down, picked up the knife, closed it, and then, with a jerk forward, scared the triplet back to the ground.

Blue turned and held the knife out to Dewey, who was back in the moment. "Here's yer prize," and then looking back at the triplet, he asked, "Ya don't minds, does ya? Nows ya can really say 'e has somethin' of yers."

After Ian shook his head and hobbled off toward his cowering group at the far end of the small parking lot, Dewey shook his head. "I... I can't have that. Mommy... mom won't let me keep it."

Blue frowned. "Don't tells 'er. Why's she have ta know anyway? Dwight, if we does everythin' our parents says we'd never grow up."

"It's a nice knife though," Dewy said, deciding to take it, admiring it, and both glad and scared to have it. Then a thought hit him. "Hey, where did you get those things you used?"

Blue lifted his pant legs to offer a peek at his bare ankles. "Ya mean my socks?" Shaking the ice out, he shoved the socks into his jacket pocket. "Okay, let's get outta 'ere."

Grinning, Stevie placed his arm over Dewey's shoulder and they walked home.

"I have to admits I was pretty worried that there was five of 'em. What abouts ya, Stevie?"

Stevie nodded his head.

Dewey smiled. "You two didn't seem worried, and, Stevie, you were even smiling."

"Stevie always smiles. The scary look doesn't work for 'im. But anyway, ya saw what I means abouts the face. They would've started in on us rights away if I didn't use 'er. Hey, singin' out loud worked this time, worked great, but next time, sing 'er in yer head. I doubts they'll fall for it again."

Dewey lost his smile. *Again!?*

When Dewey got home, he returned the five dollars to his mother and said nothing about his sharp *prize*, and since he was certain his mother would eventually come across it if he hid it in his room, he would keep it in the pocket of his pants, moving it from dirty to clean ones every morning.

CHAPTER 7
Some Adjust Better Than Others

During her first week in the new apartment, Lisa had met almost all of her first-floor neighbors and a few living on the second and third floors. The first neighbor she met was Mrs. Publicover, an elderly woman in her early seventies who wore her long gray hair up in a bun and even though she never married, referred to herself as Misses.

When Mrs. Publicover made her first attempt to meet her new neighbor by knocking on Lisa's door in the middle of the afternoon to complain about her television being too loud, Lisa apologized and told her she would turn down the volume, but she didn't. She didn't have to. The television had been off much of the day while she and Avriel painted the second coat on the living/dining room walls.

The next afternoon, when Lisa met the old woman at the door again, the woman held a small white toy poodle under one arm and said loud enough to be heard over the dog barking at Lisa, "Hellooo." Then to calm the dog, she insisted Lisa give it a small dog biscuit, which the woman carried in the pocket of her dress, and after the dog gobbled down the biscuit and stopped barking, they had to perform the task again when Avriel stopped rolling the paint to see what all the barking was about.

Hiding her annoyance, Lisa said, "I'm sorry about the TV. I'll go turn it down right now."

"Dear, I'm here to apologize to you. I think I may have come off a little too rude yesterday and I don't think it started us off on the right footing at all. I'm Mrs. Publicover and this here is Snowflake."

After Lisa introduced Avriel and herself, she explained that they were in the middle of painting the walls. "But someday soon we'll have to have coffee together."

"That would be wonderful," the old lady smiled. "And I hope you're there too, Mr. Rosen. Bye-bye, for now," she said, waving her dog's paw before she left.

Then around seven-thirty that same night, Lisa answered the door to find Mrs. Publicover holding a plate of warm tea biscuits in one hand and Snowflake in the other, and since they had quit painting for the day, Lisa reluctantly invited the seemingly harmless woman in. And as the three sat at the kitchen table, the woman released her dog, who took off barking toward Sam, who stood his ground in the living room area and calmly swiped the nose of the small dog, who yelped and ran under its mistress' chair. "Oh, I don't like that, not at all," Mrs. Publicover frowned. "Is there a room you can lock the cat in?"

"No," Avriel said.

"Oh, well, I guess we'll have to put up with it, Snowflake," the old woman said, picking up her dog and setting it on her lap.

As Lisa served coffee and all three buttered and ate the tea biscuits, Avriel said nothing. He didn't have to say anything, and Lisa didn't have to speak either. Mrs. Publicover did all the speaking. She spoke about the people in their building, starting with Frank, whom she called François and adored for both his kindness and being a responsible single father. She talked about the often drunk construction worker who lived beside François, mentioned the young girl with her newborn second child who lived across from François, and then went on for a few minutes about the two retired brothers who shared the apartment between her and the drunkard and who she initially thought were 'pansies' until they started being 'fresh' with her, which seemed to flatter her. She finished with their neighbors by mentioning the quiet girl in the apartment across from Lisa's, whose boyfriend recently went to prison for drug possession.

Mrs. Publicover was proud to have lived all of her life in Spryfield and was even prouder being the fourth generation of Publicovers to have lived there. They lived there for such a long time that a few miles further down Herring Cove Road, she owned a small parcel of land her father had gained through squatter's rights, which some company kept offering her more and more money for, but she would never sell it because it was her 'heritage.'

Then Mrs. Publicover told them how the area had changed since becoming part of the city ten years before. She went on about how they could have parties as loud as they wanted, could walk to their friend's home drunk without fear of being arrested for drunkenness, and could simply go out to the woods behind their house to shoot a deer for dinner if they chose to. "You could tell who was having venison for dinner by where the blast came from that afternoon!" Then she complained that the area had lost its tranquility when the city moved in the 'riff-raff.'

"Yes, sir, the city did nothing but designate the area Nigger Town!" said the old woman, who then pointed in the direction of the hill on the other side of Herring Cove Road. "They tried putting those monkeys out of the way up there, but we know they're there. They still find some reason or other to come down and bother us normal white folk. Hell, I've even seen them in this building!" When Avriel and Lisa's jaws dropped and they exchanged wide-eyed glances, Mrs. Publicover mistook it for empathy and continued. "If you ask me, I think they should put a wall around that hill. I mean, half of those darkies are used to prison anyway. It'd make them more comfortable, wouldn't it? At the very least, they should give them less reason to come down here. Put a store up there, maybe a mall that carries only Nigger stuff."

Avriel noticed Lisa's normally pale complexion turning red, and he tried redirecting the subject by asking, "Are there any white folks living up there?"

"Sure, but they're as black inside as the darkest Nigger."

Then Avriel tried again. "Would there be any Jews there?"

The old woman stared at him for a moment and then laughed. "Kikes? Kikes! They wouldn't be caught dead there! They're too smart... and too rich to come here. No reason for it. No, you'll never find one setting foot in Spryfield."

Lisa shot a smirk at Avriel and her face reddened even deeper, but this time it wasn't from holding in her anger, but from holding in her laughter.

"Now some folks might be glad of that. You know, bringing in the Niggers to keep out the Kikes sort of thing. Personally, I've no problem with them Kikes at all, not at all. Sure, they killed Jesus and all that, but that was a long time ago, and they didn't know any better. No, you can't knock a group for what their ancestors did. Hell, if we did that, we might all be in prison, right? Right?" Mrs. Publicover laughed again before taking on a more serious tone. "Mr. Rosen, are there any Niggers or Kikes in England?"

Unsure how to respond, Avriel said, "There are... there are quite a few Jews and Black people there."

"You have some, eh? Black people? Is that what you call

Niggers over there? I thought you folks sent all yours here two hundred years ago... not that I hold that against you personally, you understand."

Avriel was about to reply that Britain did no such thing when Dewey and Blue entered the apartment.

"Mom, I'm home," Dewey said as he and Blue kicked off their sneakers at the door and walked into the living/dining room.

"Hello, Mrs. Dixon. Hello, sir," Blue said, and then noticing Lisa's burning complexion, said, "Hey, Mrs. Publicover. Mary was just at your door."

"Mary McNeal?"

"Right... sure. She said she'd try you again in ten minutes."

"Well, Lisa, Mr. Rosen, I should be... I must be going. I haven't seen Mary in forever. You'll have to excuse my rudeness, but I don't want to miss her," she said as she placed Snowflake on the floor, stood up from the chair, and then with her dog growling and barking at Dewey, added loudly, "We'll have to continue this discussion later. I'll come back for the plate later, dear."

Lisa held the dish with the two remaining tea biscuits out to the old woman and said over the barking dog, "Here you go. No reason to make two trips. Thanks. They were great."

Reluctantly taking the dish, Mrs. Publicover walked quickly to the door with Snowflake chasing after her.

Avriel took a deep breath. "That was... uh... interesting. Thank you, Blue. Your timing was almost perfect, and twenty minutes sooner would have made it more so."

"No problem, sir, but twenty minutes sooner you wouldn't have found out how crazy she is," Blue said as he went and closed the apartment door.

"We had an idea," Lisa said. "So, Mary's her daughter?"

"I don't know. There wasn't a Mary at her door. I just said that to get rid of her. Almost everyone knows a Mary. Just like almost everybody has a Bob for an uncle. She would've stayed here forever unless you kicked her out. In ten minutes she'll forget all about Mary... and she might even forget she was here," Blue smirked.

Lisa stood up, walked over to Blue, and hugged him. "You're our hero. Thank you, Blue." Then, straightening up, she asked, "Okay, who wants ice cream?"

They all did, including Sam.

Lisa's other neighbors kept to themselves, and after her visit from Mrs. Publicover, Lisa was fine with that.

She, Avriel, and Dewey met the neighbor directly across from her, a very shy, skinny single mother of a toddler. The teen mother welcomed Lisa to the building and introduced herself and her daughter, Samantha, before quickly entering her apartment. Then, while bringing her folded clothes from the laundry room, she passed the construction worker, who mumbled something incoherent under his breath and was still fumbling with his keys when she entered her apartment. Then one afternoon, while leaving her apartment to go to work, she passed Frank in the hall talking to the two portly brothers, and when he introduced her, they greeted her in unison while eyeing her up and down. She couldn't be sure, but as she made her way up the stairs, she thought she heard one of them refer to her as *chicky*. And on the weekend, she met the mother of two. She introduced herself and received a "Yeah, whatever," as the young woman struggled to bring her children up the metal stairs.

The one neighbor Avriel, Lisa, and Dewey would continue to bump into would be Art. They first met him one evening when they were leaving the apartment and had to pass him single file as he sat on the concrete steps carving something from a block of wood. When Dewey introduced them, Art seemed shy, but when Dewey asked what he was carving, he seemed to relax, telling them it was an elephant and what part he was going to be working on that evening. As the three walked toward Avriel's car, he told them not to worry about his mess of wood chips. "That's why I brings out that there broom and dustpan there. Don't wanna upsets Cawland again."

**

By the end of that first week, Lisa and Avriel finished their painting, replaced the missing toilet cover, installed a peephole in the apartment door, though purposely lower than the average height, attached Dewey's bookshelf to his bedroom wall, put up his posters, and hung several of his model jet fighters from its ceiling.

Working early or not, each morning Lisa walked Dewey to school, and as per Dewey's request, they parted at the grocery store so he could walk the last bit on his own. Also, as per his request, Lisa reluctantly stopped holding his hand. She assumed both requests were because of his maturing, and that was the reason for his not wanting to hold hands, but the reason for his wanting to walk alone from the grocery store was because of his classmates commenting on how pretty she was. Even though it made him popular, it bothered him to hear his mother referred to as pretty. 'The pretty lady' wasn't how he saw his mother, but he would have to admit she was prettier than most of the other mothers he had seen.

Lisa was comfortable letting Dewey walk the last block to school alone. Herring Cove Road was a busy street during the morning rush hour and any person stalking children there would have a difficult if not an impossible time operating there during that time of the day.

When alone, Lisa's mind was consistently on the Kid Killer and she found it strange how everyone around her seemed to have forgotten about it even though there was still at least one killer out there. Avriel didn't mention it. Frank didn't mention it, and even Mrs. Publicover didn't mention it. It was as if the subject became taboo. They found the body of the second child about a month back and perhaps that was enough time for some to forget about the horrific event. Maybe she would've forgotten about it too if the police had caught the killer or killers, but while the killer was still out there, her concern was still there.

Lisa felt certain one person was doing the killings. She couldn't accept more than one person being capable of it, and she was sure it was a man, since she couldn't accept a woman doing such a thing. With each man she met, she might consider them a potential suspect and put them, if only temporarily, on her mental suspect list, and in her building alone, she had three men still on the list. She was realistic enough to know she might be being irrational, but as long as it didn't hurt or embarrass anyone, she felt it was best to be so.

**

Unlike at his old school, Dewey didn't bring lunch. Avriel picked him up from school every lunch period, taking him to a restaurant, sometimes back to Lisa's apartment to have lunch with her when she wasn't working, and sometimes to his own house for sandwiches.

The first month after the move, Avriel spent much of his time at the Dixons', but because of Dewey's new friends, he was spending only a short time with the boy, so at the end of the second week of April and with his relatively recent fondness for television, he surprised Lisa and Dewey with a housewarming gift of a floor-model color television, which she thought was too much, and the next week he had cable television installed with the hoped it would entice Dewey and his friends to hang out in the apartment more often.

Even with all the time he was spending at the Dixons', the first month after the move was a time of renewed anxiety for him. He had a tough time adjusting to them not being just next door, and he came to dislike being alone outside in front of his home, where he felt much like the Hunchback of Notre Dame.

As the warmer weather gave him more reason to be outside, Avriel noticed his neighbors' coldness toward him. He first noticed it when he was painting his green front door white. As several neighbors walked by, he tried being neighborly by greeting them, but if they even recognized his greetings, they were received frigidly. Most of the responses were non-verbal, involving only a subtle acknowledgment of his existence through a small gesture like a slight wave of the hand from the person's hip, a forced smile, or with Mr. Smith from across the street, the only other person on the street besides the Dixons who Avriel had talked to, a nod from an almost expressionless face. Avriel even suspected some of his neighbors of crossing the street just to avoid him. It seemed to happen mostly with mothers and their infants, and it seemed to happen too often to be just in his head. Then one early afternoon, his neighbor's coldness was further confirmed when he brought Dewey to his home for lunch and the boy's greetings to his neighbors passing by were also ignored or barely acknowledged, much as Avriel had first reacted when Dewey repeatedly greeted him as Mr. Jew, mistaking his father's reference to the "Jews next door" as their last name. Avriel even found himself questioning if the message spray-painted on his front door the previous summer was done by someone other than Paul Dixon.

Avriel found it strange that his neighbors were distancing themselves from him over what he considered a silly rumor of an affair between him and Lisa, but then when he forced himself to think about the events of the previous eight months, he could see several more substantial reasons. There was him hitting Dewey with his car, or rather, Dewey hitting Avriel's car with his bike. There was the commotion caused by Paul Dixon when Lisa had locked him out of the house, leading to a fight between him and Avriel and the death of Avriel's wife. There was Paul Dixon's accidental death in Avriel's home when he was trying to kill Avriel, and there was his discovering the small body of the first victim that previous fall. Avriel expected that even though all of that had been out of his control, it would still be enough to turn people away from him, but what he failed to consider was that when he and his wife had first moved onto the street, the extreme introversion he had practiced by keeping to himself and letting his wife speak for him had put off many of the residents, creating their first bad impression of him, and everything after that added to it.

Being ostracized by his neighbors increased Avriel's anxiety, and at times, that anxiety took a toll on his patience.

The Canadian government had adopted the metric system and by mid-April of that year, they began changing the road signs from miles per hour to kilometers per hour, exciting Dewey. At his new school, he had learned to convert kilometers per hour to miles per hour and vice versa, and he grabbed the chance to show off his new knowledge by converting the kilometer speed limit signs into miles. As a fifty-kilometer posting approached, he would tell Avriel to go thirty miles an hour, and then closely watch the speedometer, commenting every few seconds with, "You're going almost fifty-five kilometers now," or, "Now you're going too slow. You're only at forty-five kilometers." Then, after several dozen of Dewey's conversions, Avriel tried beating him to the punch by calling out the mile conversions himself, but that didn't stop the boy from monitoring and commenting on the car's speed. Finally, having had enough of Dewey's *help*, Avriel asked, "Dewey, do you know why the States have not adopted the metric system?"

"No, why?"

"Because they are waiting to see how far the Canadian child mortality rate rises because of it. That is what the *kil* part of kilometer stands for."

After Lisa laughed, she told Dewey to climb over to the back seat, and as he did, he commented he was sure *Kilo* stood for a thousand, and once on the back seat, he asked, "What's a child mortality rate?"

His mother smirked. "If you don't be quiet, you'll find out the hard way."

Disappointed, Dewey did as he was told. He knew by then that nothing good ever came from finding out the hard way.

By the middle of April, Avriel felt Lisa could use some alone time, so he purchased a television game called Pong for his home, and each Sunday evening, he and Dewey would sit on the floor in front of the old man's floor model television and spin their controllers' dial to move their small pixilated paddles up and down the screen, blocking the square puck coming at them and sending it back to the other side. Then, so they could do something as a group, Avriel came up with Saturday movie night, which included Stevie and Blue, who always insisted on paying for his and Stevie's tickets and snacks, and each Saturday night, the five of them would travel to one of four cinemas, depending on where the movie played.

Stevie's mother, Mrs. Kelly, always gave her permission, but she didn't want her son walking in the dark, even from just the parking lot to his door, and she refused to burden Avriel and Lisa with walking him, so after each movie, Lisa would use a pay phone at the cinema to call her and let her know they were on their way and when they should arrive back. It could be only minutes if they went to the cinema in the Spryfield Mall or it could be as long as thirty if they went as far as downtown to the Paramount Cinema on Barrington Street, and after driving up Carson Street and turning left onto the first street, they would find the mother standing in the parking lot surrounded by Orange Walk's townhouses. Lisa thought she was being considerate, but the real reason was that it would embarrass her to have them see inside her townhouse. With four boys, her house was always in disarray.

Everyone looked forward to movie night, and to keep order with the three excited boys, Avriel and Lisa would sit behind them, Lisa making it her job to interrupt them when their talking and joking threatened to disturb the others around them and Avriel making it his job to do the reverse. At least once during each movie, Avriel wound up the boys by whispering comments from behind them. He started during their first movie night. Close to the end of the showing of the classic 1933 movie, *The Invisible Man*, Avriel leaned forward into the boys and asked, "Where's the Invincible Man?"

"You can't see him. He's invisible," Dewey told him.

"Oh, so he's both invincible and invisible?"

"No, he's just invisible. He's the Invisible Man, not the Invincible Man."

Feigning disappointment, Avriel said, "Oh... I–I suppose I must have read it wrong. I was hoping to see an invincible man, and I can't even see this guy who is not even invincible!"

The boys broke up laughing and then laughed more at their inappropriate laughing.

During their second movie night, they watched a western. When a brawl broke out in a bar and in his best western accent, which the boys found funny by itself, Avriel whispered, "I feels real sorely for whoevers gots ta clean up this 'ere darn mess." While the audience silently watched the fight, the three boys laughed through it. Each time a table smashed, a mirror or a window shattered or a beer mug was smashed over someone's head, Avriel would exclaim through a whisper, "Darn it!" or, "That's me favorite glass!" or, "Here comes another seven years of bad luck!" or, "Me father done gives me that before he ups and died... and that there too... and that too!" causing the boys to laugh louder.

Avriel's reward for causing the commotion was Lisa's shoe to his shin, and the old comedian soon learned to pack paper napkins into his socks before each movie, which he would forget about until getting ready for bed, causing his nightstand to accumulate an impressive pile of wrinkled paper napkins.

By early May, Avriel decided he had had enough of his neighborhood. If he were going to be seen as the street's crazy old man, it would be much easier for him to move rather than prove he wasn't. Deciding to move back to Jubilee Road, where he had lived for almost twenty years before his wife had moved them to Gilmore Street, he talked to Lisa's real estate agent about selling his house, and about his plan to buy Lisa's anonymously at its asking price to relieve her of some of her stress, and Lisa's agent couldn't have been happier. The real estate agent would be making four transactions from the old man: the selling of three on Gilmore (selling Lisa's again after Avriel had purchased it) and Avriel's purchase of one in a much more expensive neighborhood.

There were only large houses on Jubilee Road, very large houses, and Avriel was comfortable with the larger, secluded properties, but he didn't expect to be comfortable living in one alone and hoped Lisa and Dewey would join him. They could all live in a much larger house in a better neighborhood, have enough yard space to enjoy during the summer, and Dewey could have enough bedroom space to hold sleepovers with his new friends. Avriel even considered that he could install an in-ground pool if he failed to find a house with one.

Several times a day, Avriel found himself planning how to approach the subject with Lisa. How could he convince her she wouldn't be giving up her independence? Then one evening, while Dewey was out with Blue, she excitedly informed him about her house selling at her asking price, with the sale closing only days after she had signed the papers that coming week, and after paying off the balance of her mortgage, she would have substantial savings in the bank. With that and her hopes of a promotion to Head Cashier in the next month, she could afford a larger apartment after her current one-year lease was up.

Avriel faked his surprise well, and after letting her know how happy he was for her, he saw his opportunity and took it, starting by telling her how he was making plans to move to Jubilee Road. Lisa knew the road. Everyone knew the road. It was one of the few posh areas in Halifax outside of the South End. But the only hesitation he had, he told her, was the size of the houses there. It just seemed wrong to live alone in such a large house, and he wondered if she might be interested in living there with him. With all the time they were spending together, they were almost living together as it was. Then he tried to assure her she would still have her independence, and he mentioned they could even hire a housekeeper, since the house's size would be too much for either of them to want to clean. Not seeing a positive response in her eyes — it was more of a surprise — Avriel pulled the sympathy card by adding he was getting to the age where in the future he may need help now and then and would benefit from the arrangement as much as she would, if not more.

Lisa was silent for several seconds, which seemed like minutes to Avriel, and when she finally spoke, she told him she liked the idea but thought a move to another neighborhood may be too soon for Dewey, who had adjusted well to the move. He had made friends, had started a new school, and was rapidly maturing from the experience, and she wouldn't feel right forcing him to start another school and have to make new friends. Then she explained that when she had talked about moving to a larger apartment, she was talking about one within the same area.

Avriel was disappointed, but he understood her concerns and couldn't understand why he hadn't thought about Dewey's situation. Perhaps his desire blinded him to the reality of the situation. Perhaps he was being self-centered. Then, just as Sam would do when Avriel caught him digging into one of Lisa's many plants, Avriel looked everywhere but at her. He wished he were more like Ruth. She would've seen all the factors, and she would've found a better way to bring up the proposal. But then, he thought, she mightn't have agreed with him. She most likely would've agreed with Lisa and wouldn't have looked for an opportunity to present the proposal.

Seeing Avriel's disappointment, Lisa ended the conversation by giving her friend some hope for the future, telling him there was a possibility of it happening down the road, but she would need more time to ponder the idea and perhaps they should approach it again in another eight or nine months, with Dewey included in the conversation.

**

With Avriel's help, Dewey had proudly used his savings to purchase and wrap a silver necklace with a small locket containing a tiny picture of him, and on the morning of the second Sunday of May, he presented his mother with a

Mother's Day card and the gift. Lisa was more than surprised, but when he volunteered to make breakfast, she suggested that if he was set on doing it, then that could be his next year's Mother's Day gift.

With Dewey at Avriel's home on Sunday evenings, making those nights Lisa's nights alone, she usually took a bubble bath, and sometimes while soaking the stress away, would drink a glass of red wine while reading a romance novel or a woman's magazine, but that Mother's Day evening was different. Until that time, Lisa and Frank had only talked in passing, where Frank usually ended their brief conversations with a half-joke about them getting away from the boys for an evening, and on Mother's Day evening, they did. It was Lisa's first actual date since she felt she had never dated her husband (they simply hung out together until she discovered she was pregnant and they got married) and to make certain she'd be home in time for Dewey's return from Avriel's, she told Avriel of her plans and asked him if he would bring Dewey home later than normal, around eleven. Even though he didn't know Frank well enough *not* to be suspicious of him, Avriel was happy for her and would drop off Dewey later than usual and oblivious to his mother's date.

Dressed in a suit, Frank took a flattered Lisa out to dinner and then, at the end of the night and after finishing a bottle of wine, made her promise to do the same for him on Father's Day.

That following Sunday, as Lisa was filling the bathtub with bubble bath, she answered a knock on her apartment door to find Frank standing there holding flowers and a bottle of red wine. Flattered again, she invited her romantic neighbor in.

CHAPTER 8
The Three Musketeers

On his first day at his new school, Dewey didn't bother correcting his teachers as he normally would when they addressed him as Dwight, so all called him by his given name, but not yet used to being called it, during that first week his teachers and classmates had to call out to him several times before he realized they were calling to him, making it a stressful adjustment for him. After three or four calls to him, the person's frustration showed in their voice and they might call out to him as Dwight Dixon, causing him some stress. He had been conditioned that when he heard his first and last name yelled out in frustration, he was in trouble, but less trouble than if it also included his middle name.

Dewey made friends at school easier than he had expected, but with Blue and Stevie as his best buddies, he placed little weight on his new school friends. Like his last school, he didn't see his classmates outside of it — he lived too far away — and at the end of that first week, he decided he wanted to switch to Blue and Stevie's school, and he would try to persuade his mother to change schools the next school year. If he couldn't persuade her, he figured Blue could try, and if Blue failed, he could probably recruit Avriel to try as well. He knew better than to have Stevie try.

Spending his evenings and weekends hanging out with Blue and Stevie, Dewey learned his new friends only drank beer and smoked cigarettes at the graveyard on Saturdays, and on the occasional weeknights, they went to Roi des Arbres just to hang out away from everything.

Because of the giant pine tree standing in the middle of a large circular clearing walled in by densely packed thinner trees, Blue had named the spot Roi des Arbres, naming it in French because "Everythin' sounds better in French." Situated deep in the woods at the end of Autumn Drive, Roi des Arbres was closer to home, and since there was no path near it, it was more secluded than the graveyard and the perfect place to explode small bits of cordite.

Blue would get some cordite from a classmate who got it from Portuguese Cove (or Cordite Cove, as it was nicknamed), which was much further down Herring Cove Road. Many tiny pieces of cordite about the size of a pencil's eraser still washed up on the rocky shore from the ships that had sunk off the coast decades earlier, and all one had to do was reach down and pick them up. With the cordite dried, the boys would smash it between two rocks, creating a bang as loud as a gunshot, but would barely make it through the forest and onto Autumn Drive.

To ensure he had time to hang out with his friends in the evening, Dewey began doing his homework before supper rather than after it, and sometimes Stevie would bring his math homework to Roi des Arbres to have Dewey or Blue help him with it, but Blue wouldn't. He thought it best that Dewey help Stevie since Dewey was one year ahead of him and, "The stuff's still fresh in yer head." But Dewey found the homework was stuff he had done two years earlier. Blue might bring his homework with him too, but he did little of it, choosing instead to watch a frustrated Dewey doing his friend's homework. Stevie and he would sit next to each other on a bed of pine needles, and with his arm over Dewey's shoulder, Stevie would nod and repeat, "Uh huh," as Dewey explained what he was doing while he worked out each problem.

More than watching Dewey getting suckered into doing Stevie's math homework, Blue enjoyed watching the two's training sessions, cheering on one or the other, or sometimes both at the same time. In return for 'helping' him with his homework, Stevie silently showed Dewey how to fistfight. He showed him the proper way to make a fist, how to stand, how to punch, where to punch, and various combinations of punches, and after a few training sessions, when Stevie felt Dewey was ready, they sparred, but instead of using fists, they tapped each other with open hands. Initially, Dewey was too nervous and barely able to touch Stevie, but after several sessions of sparring, he relaxed and could land more taps.

Blue's courting continued to fascinate Dewey. On their second Saturday together, as the three sat on their swings slightly buzzed and waiting for the sisters, Blue said to no one, "What's it, really? We can't sees it, yet we knows it's there. We can feels it, yet we can't touch it. It doesn't live, but it grows. Why do we feels it for one and not everyone? And when we feels it for different people, it's gots different strengths. Why the hell does it gots ta be so damn complicated!?"

Startling Dewey, Stevie grabbed the chain of his swing and pulled him closer, and startling him again, he whispered in his ear, "What de'ell's lover boy talkin' aboot?" Dewey didn't know and had no time to relay the question. Just at that moment, Blue spotted the sisters coming down the street, slid off his seat, and took off toward them. When he reached them and said a few words to the smaller sister, the taller one again pushed him down and again kicked him, but this time the smaller sister just stood there watching. When the taller one finished, both girls took off.

The following Saturday, as expected, the taller sister pushed Blue down again, but then the smaller sister pushed her away before she could start kicking him, and after the smaller one had helped him up, she was off to join her sister.

Dewey then realized what Stevie already knew. Blue was letting them knock him down, and he was letting them kick him too, and Dewey was beginning to believe Blue had lost his mind.

The next time they waited for the sisters, the smaller one stopped her sister before she could knock Blue down and said something to her that caused her to run off. Grabbing Blue, the girl aggressively hugged him, kissed his cheek, and said something to him before taking off after her sister.

Then, with a huge smile and a skip in his step, Blue returned to the swings, gave a thumbs-up, and said, "Yeah! First base!"

Dewey didn't know what Blue meant, and he had no time to ask. The girls assaulting his friend became his reminder that they had to rush home for supper and then a movie.

The next day at Avriel's house, Dewey asked him what *first base* meant, startling the old man, who hadn't expected such a question to come for a couple of more years. "Uh... that is when a boy and girl kiss on the lips, or it used to be."

"You ever get to first base?"

"I believe so. It was some time ago, so it is difficult to remember. I was married, so I expect I have. Have you met a special girl?"

"No," Dewy said, without the defensiveness he might have had if he had been asked the summer before.

For the first time, Dewey thought Avriel could be wrong. He saw the smaller sister kiss Blue on the cheek, not the lips, and yet Blue called it *first base*. Or perhaps they were both correct. Perhaps it didn't matter where the kiss went, but it had to be with a girl; otherwise, Dewey would've gotten to first base with his mother, and that just didn't seem right.

Unbeknownst to Lisa and Avriel, after supper and while the promotion of the free bags of potato chips lasted, the three boys would eat their fill of chips while occasionally hanging out at the corner store, where Dewey learned there was always one of three people working in it: there was Mr. Delaney, whom he had met his first time there, there was Mr. Delaney's wife, a tall, quiet woman who stood a foot taller than her husband, and there was Mr. Mumphy who, Blue told Dewy, used to be a gym teacher at one of the nearby schools until they fired him for smacking students. Sometimes, Blue would refer to Mr. Mumphy as Mr. Grumpy and, at other times, as Mr. *Dum*phy, but only behind his back. Once, as they stood outside the door eating their chips, Mr. Mumphy came out carrying a garbage bag and a stick with a nail at the tip and demanding to know, "Who's goin' to help me clean up this place?"

Dewey instantly had a flashback to what Avriel's wife had taught him the summer before regarding a token sum: *Fifty cents is a small fee and if you charge nothing, you could end up mowing all the lawns for free. No, Dewey, you have to charge a token sum at the very minimum.* "For fifty cents, sir," he said.

Mr. Mumphy glared at Dewey for a second before looking coldly at Stevie and holding out the garbage bag and the stick.

"Fifty cents," Stevie said, putting out the palm of his hand.

Standing there confused for a moment, the man huffed,

flashed Dewey another glare, and returned to the store.

Blue laughed. "That was too cool. If ya didn't says nothin' Stevie would've ended up doin' it. He can't says no ta adults."

With Stevie shaking his head, Blue said, "It's true, and ya knows it!"

Besides being confident and streetwise, or perhaps because of it, Blue seemed to know almost everyone in the neighborhood. When a child, youth, and even an adult entered the store, they greeted Blue. Black, Asian, or White, almost all knew him. Sometimes they would stop and exchange a few words, and once Dewey was surprised to hear a tall, thin Black youth, maybe fifteen years old, greet Blue with, "Hey, Nigger, what's happenin'?" and Blue, taking his friend's hand with what initially looked like a handshake but ended with what appeared to be a dance of their fingers, responded with, "Not much, Nigger. Hangin' with me boys." When Blue introduced Dewey, the boy didn't know what to say, so he said nothing and did the head nod, as others often did.

After the youth left, Dewey said, "You called each other the N-word. Mom hates the N-word."

Blue nodded. "Yeah, yer mom's cool that way. We use Nig... the N-word fer respect. They calls me it ta say I'm one a 'em, and I calls 'em it because I'm expected ta return the compliment, but only if they uses it first. If any other honky uses it, they'd beats the shit out of 'im fer sure. It's best not ta use it... not at all. I only uses it in the proper *contest*. Isn't that rights, Stevie?"

Stevie just smiled.

At the graveyard the week after Blue had gotten to *first base*, he didn't bring the straining plastic bag. The potato chip promotion had ended and there would be no beer or cigarettes that day. The three just sat on the wall while Blue talked about his new girlfriend, whom he met at the playground for a short time each day after school. When he asked Dewey if he had seen her at his school, Dewey said he did. She hung out with several other girls, including her sister. But he didn't mention he had a crush on one of the girls. A girl one year older and heavier set than the others. Something about her had caught Dewey's interest. It could've been her light-brown hair that hung down to her waist, or her two different colored eyes, one blue and one gray, or her many freckles, or it could've been a combination of it all.

Dewey asked, "So what do you guys do?"

"We talks a little and kisses a lot."

"You kiss? Seriously?"

"Sure. We do it just in the woods behind the playground. And Frank was right when 'e taught me how. We tried different ways, and she thinks Frank's is the best."

"Frank taught you how to kiss? Seriously?"

Blue smirked. "Sure, he showed me how to makes my hand flat and press my thumb up against the side of the first finger, like this." Blue held up his hand with his fingers straight and tight together as if he was making the popular karate chop. "And then ya kiss the bit of puffed up flesh there betweens the thumb and the finger. It sorta looks like lips, right?" Blue said before he placed his lips on the bump of flesh. "See, just like that."

Curious, Dewey puckered up and kissed his hand's bump of flesh, and Stevie did the same.

"Stevie, don't suck on it. Just lightly rub yer lips over it. Dwight, don't pucker up like yer goin' to give 'er a raspberry. Guys leave yer mouth open a bit and slide yer lips gently over 'er lips. Not too rough... gentle like."

After a minute of watching and commenting on Stevie and

Dewey kissing their hands, Blue said, "Maybe it'll be easier if ya guys practices on each other."

Stevie stopped kissing his hand, made a sarcastic smile, and flipped Blue a couple of birds, and Dewey did the same.

After Blue laughed and Stevie gave Dewey a high-five, Dewey asked, "We aren't drinking and smoking today?"

"Nah, I got all the courage I needed. We're on the wagon," Blue said, with Stevie nodding in agreement.

"Not smoking either?"

"Nah, we only smoked because, as Frank says, we can't do one without the other."

"But why did *we* drink if *you* needed the... the courage?"

Blue grinned. "Cause it's not cool ta drink alone. We'll do it again. Maybe we'll drinks a case of beer together. Hey, maybe one night, when we plays a board game, we'll drinks and smoke."

Dewey followed Stevie's nodding of the head but thought if he drank more than one beer or smoked more than one cigarette, he was sure to get caught, get caught doing something he hated. It would be like getting punished twice. Besides the bad taste, he didn't like that beer made him sleepy after making him slightly disoriented, and he hated smoking and thought people only did it to be cool.

Dewey was delighted to discover his new friends enjoyed playing board games, and when they played them, it was always at Blue's place. The first time they played one was on the second Sunday morning of April when it was raining hard. With Blue insisting they hang out at his place, Dewey brought his Monopoly game from home, and after Blue had made a neat pile of the newspapers and magazines scattered about the leather sofa, loveseat, and glass-topped coffee table and had put the empty beer bottles, dirty plates, and dirty glasses in the kitchen, they set the game up on the coffee table and sat around it sharing a large bowl of potato chips and drinking their preferred flavors of Pop Shoppe soda.

As they got into the game and the properties were almost all purchased, Stevie started swearing loudly, usually, "Shit!" but sometimes, "Christ!" And when Blue started using the same expletives, Dewey figured out why he wanted to play at his place, and to fit in he started swearing too, which amused Stevie, who high-fived him the first few times he did. Dewey found he enjoyed swearing, if only because it was taboo, and the three got to swearing so often that Frank, who was sitting on the sofa and watching television, joked, "The game should've been called, "Shit! Christ! Shit!" The three boys laughed, with Dewey laughing only to hide his embarrassment at being caught swearing by an adult. He had gotten so into the game that he had forgotten Frank was sitting there. And when Blue tried adding to the joke by saying, "The French version could be called Marde! Criss! Marde!" only Frank laughed. Stevie and Dewey had to take a couple of seconds to get the joke and when they figured it out, it had lost its humor.

During the game, each time the ear-piercing buzz of the apartment's intercom sounded, Frank would answer it and then meet his friends at the door with a small paper lunch bag. The number of friends who dropped by just to greet him and get some food amazed Dewey. They seldom came in past the door, and when they did, they seldom greeted the boys. Only Tim came in and sat down, but instead of taking a seat on the sofa, he joined Stevie on the floor.

"Hey, guys! How's it goin' there, Mr. Nixon?"

"It's Dixon, sir."

"Right, right... no relation to Richard. Gots it. So, who's winnin'?"

"I think it's close. Dwight and I gots three full sets, and

Stevie gots two."

"Well, how abouts I help Stevie then?"

Stevie, who had just rolled the dice, nodded his head to Tim's offer, moved his playing piece of a metal dog, and said, "Shit!" as he landed on a property owned by Dewey.

While helping Steve, Tim took over as banker and occasionally *assisted* Stevie by sliding him some extra money and helping him move his piece around the board, usually placing Stevie's piece just before or after a spot owned by one of the other two, and when Stevie switched from swearing to laughing, Tim told him he was his lucky charm.

Stevie knew Tim was cheating. Blue knew it, and Dewey knew it too, but because of the game's excitement wearing off, no one bothered calling Tim out on it, except Frank. After Tim said, "Jesus, we need a five. Jesus, we need a five. Jesus Christ, we need a five," Frank told him to stop cursing and set a better example for the boys.

With an innocent face, Tim looked up from the board game and said, "Frank, I'm settin' a good example. I'm praying."

Only Stevie laughed.

With Blue deciding the game was over, the boys didn't bother adding up their properties and money to determine who won. They just put away the game.

Then Tim helped himself to the Manwiches Frank had made for the boys' supper, and after eating, left with a paper bag, but not before slapping five with Stevie and telling Blue and Dewey they sucked at the game.

Dewey wasn't comfortable around Tim. He found the long-haired skinny man strange for an adult, like a weird kid in a man's body, and one Saturday afternoon, when Blue told him Tim was driving him and Stevie to the Simpsons Mall and he was welcome to come along, Dewey was reluctant to go, and when he asked his mother, hoping she would say no, she disappointed him by giving her permission, five dollars, and a wish to have a good time. Lisa never met Tim, but she thought if Frank would allow it, Tim could be trusted.

During the drive, Tim was unusually quiet as he followed Herring Cove Road to the Armdale Rotary, passed through half of it, and then flew up the hill on the opposite side. With squealing tires, he made a hard left into a parking lot and skidded to a stop at the Sears entrance, causing the boys to slide forward. With no goodbyes, the three got out and headed toward the double doors, and a second later, with an impatient squeal of tires, Tim was gone.

Dewey stopped at the doors. "Hey, where are you going?"

"In," Blue said, holding the door open.

"Shouldn't we wait for Tim?"

"Nope, he's not comin'."

"But I told my mom he was taking us!"

With some impatience, Blue said, "He took us, and now he's gone."

Dewey stood there for a moment, wondering and worrying if he had lied to his mother. If he did it by accident, would that still count as a lie?

"Ya comin'!?" Blue asked with more impatience.

Realizing there was nowhere else to go and then finding himself thankful that Tim wasn't there with them, Dewey said, "Yeah, I'm... I'm coming."

The boys walked through Sears, took the escalator up to the next level, and left the store to enter the mall.

Dewey recognized the mall. He had gone there with his parents, but they had always entered on the other side of the building where it looked different because of its much larger parking lot and its row of buses and taxis lining its nine-foot-wide sidewalk.

The three made their way down the wide, marble-tiled hall, passing several clothing stores, a couple of shoe stores, a Carlton Bookstore, and a Craig's Pharmacy before Blue made a left into The Tobacco King.

At the counter, when Blue asked to see the Zippo lighters, the long-haired, sparsely bearded salesclerk, who to Dewey looked like Shaggy from the Scooby Doo cartoons, eyed Blue with suspicion. "Ya just lookin' or ya buyin'?"

"Buyin'," Blue said, pulling a handful of bills from his pocket and holding them up. "Ya just showin' or ya sellin'?"

"Sellin'," the salesclerk said, after glancing at the entrance of the store where several people were passing.

When he pulled out a tray of Zippo lighters, Blue saw the one he wanted and pointed to a larger Zippo with an engraving of a marijuana leaf on it. "How much?"

"Twelve ninety-nine."

"Flints and fuel?"

"Sixteen forty-seven plus tax."

"Make it fifteen and I'll take 'em without no receipt," Blue said, causing Dewey's jaw to drop.

The salesclerk chuckled. "Damn, kid, it's a deal. Ya gives a tough bargain."

Dewey looked over at Stevie to see his reaction, and not seeing one, he watched Blue count out fifteen dollars and hand it to the salesclerk, who handed him a plastic bag. Then following Blue out of the store, he asked, "I thought you had to be older to buy a lighter? And how did you get all that money?"

"Ya has to be fifteen. Frank gives me money each week. I just saves what I don't spends. Did ya see the guy's long hair? They're called hippies. Frank once told me that guys with long hair don't like rules, don't likes status *quotes*, and don't follow 'em. So last month, when I saw 'im workin' there, I knew that was my in fer Frank's birthday present."

As they continued further down the mall, Dewey began looking for long-haired men. He saw a few and thought it interesting how a person could identify the rule breakers by the length of their hair. He thought it interesting too that the hippies would advertise their propensity for breaking rules by growing their hair long. It must make it easy to catch them, he thought.

Almost at the end of the mall, across from the food court and a couple of dozen feet away from the entrance to The Hudson Bay department store, the three stopped at Mahon's Stationery, where Blue gave some money to Stevie and told him to pick out four birthday cards, some wrapping paper and a small gift box, describing the dimensions with his hands.

With Stevie gone, Blue and Dewey planted themselves on a bench to wait.

"You don't like picking out cards?" Dewey asked as shoppers walked past them in both directions.

"Yeah, but not allowed in there."

"Huh? Why?"

"Last time I wasn't quick enough, and they nabbed me. Frank grounded me for almost a month. I was *confided* to the apartment... until he wents to work."

"Quick enough for what?"

"Fer stealin'"

"You tried to steal something?"

"Yeah. Don't look so shocked, man. I'm sure ya stole somethin' before," Blue said defensively.

"No! Never!"

"Not nothin'?"

"Nothing, ever!"

"Damn, ya really ares a goodie-goodie."

Dewey didn't know if he should be proud, embarrassed, or offended, so he said nothing as he looked at the floor.

"There's nothin' wrongs with bein' a goodie-goodie, except maybe that it's borin'," Blue said as put his arm around Dewey's shoulder. "Stevie's a goodie-goodie too, but that's mainly because he can't talk 'is way outta anythin'. Ya gets it? He can't talk 'is way outta anythin'," Blue said, nudging Dewey. "Ya gets it?"

Dewey laughed and then Blue laughed, and when both realized they were laughing at Stevie, not with him, they stopped laughing to wait in silence for their friend.

They only had to wait a few minutes more before Stevie returned with an orange plastic bag in his hand. Handing it and the change to Blue, he sat down on the other side of him.

Taking out the cards, Blue read the first one. "*To a wonderful father, Happy Birthday from a wonderful son.* That's cool!" Then he looked at the next card. "*Be careful with your cake. At your age, it's a fire hazard. Happy Birthday!* Cool. Yers or—" After Stevie nodded, he read the third card, "*One more year and another foot closer to the grave. Happy Birthday... anyway!*" Laughing, he passed the card to Dewey, who read it and laughed at the picture of a gravestone with a birthday cake resting on top of it.

Blue looked at Stevie. "That's fer Tim ta give?"

Stevie shook his head and pointed to Dewey, who stopped laughing, which made Blue laugh again, but louder, causing shoppers to notice.

Blue collected himself. "Okay, the last one. *Happy Birthday! I know this card isn't much, but then neither are you.*"

With all three laughing, Blue was the first to stop and said, "Stevie, Tim's goin' ta be pissed!"

Then when Stevie whispered in his ear, Blue roared with

more laughter.

"What did he say? What did he say?" Dewey begged.

Blue forced himself to stop laughing, wiped his eyes with his hands, and said, "Not as much as Frank."

With Dewey laughing hard, Stevie grinned proudly.

"You boys having fun?"

The three turned their heads to a man standing behind them with his arms crossed as he glared down at them. Sporting a buzz cut that seemed to beg for respect, he wore a gray uniform a size too big with a patch on its shoulder that read Mall Security.

Standing up to face the man, Blue held up the two bags and said, "Yes, sir. We're out shopping and enjoying it."

Unimpressed, the security guard said, "Well good, maybe you guys can pretend you're in public and use your inside voices. Remember, you're not at home!"

"Yes, sir. We will, sir. Sorry, sir."

"Okay, I'll be watching you three," warned the guard, who then turned to walk away. Stopping, he turned around and asked, "What did you buy?"

"Some Birthday cards."

The guard put out his hand, and Blue handed over the orange bag, and after the guard looked inside, he handed it back. "And the other bag?"

Blue hesitated.

"Let's see the other one."

When Blue reluctantly handed it over, the Guard peered into it. "You fifteen?"

Blue nodded.

"You got I.D.?"

Blue shook his head.

"Then I'm confiscating the lighter and stuff," the guard smirked, and when Blue put on his scary face, his smirk grew to a smile. "It'll be at the security station. Your parents can pick it up there. You boys have a great day now," the guard said as he squeezed the bag into his pants pocket and again turned to walk away.

Blue sat back down between Stevie and Dewey and for almost a minute, the three said nothing until Blue said, "Damn, cop wannabees! Okay, let's get somethin' to eat. It's on me."

At the food court, they lined up at the A&W counter, and after Blue paid, each carried their tray of a burger, fries and a drink to an empty metal table firmly bolted to the floor, sat themselves down on hard plastic seats also bolted to the floor, and ate in silence.

When they had finished eating and were slurping the last of their drinks, Blue said, "Let's hit the road," but after Stevie whispered in his ear, he said, "But let's hit the can first."

With Dewey following behind, Stevie and Blue entered a corridor behind the food court, and stopping a door short of the men's washroom, Blue pushed open a door that read MEN'S WASHROOM -MALL PERSONNEL ONLY and all three entered.

The washroom was in almost pristine condition. Covered in white ceramic tile, its walls were almost spotless except for a bit of graffiti below the Please Wash Your Hands sign taped above the two porcelain sinks built into the counter. A urinal and a stall were to their right.

With Stevie standing in front of the urinal while Blue entered the stall beside it, Dewey waited, and after a few seconds, Blue returned and Dewey entered the stall.

Dewey had zipped up his fly and was about to flush when he heard someone enter and say, "So, you're trespassing too, are you? You know I didn't recognize you as that stationary thief until after I talked to you little shits. So you're doing some vandalizing too are you, like maybe that there writing above the sink."

"That wasn't us, ya... ya minimum wage copsucker!" Blue protested.

Cautiously, Dewey peeked out of the stall to see the mall guard from earlier.

"You two stay where you are," the guard demanded as he looked over at Dewey and Stevie, who had to force himself to stop peeing. "Cocksucker am I?" he asked Blue as he grabbed him by his armpits and set him on the counter.

"I don't knows anythin' abouts that. I just knows yer a *cop*sucker!", Blue said, and when the guard grabbed him by the shirt, he yelled, "Help! Help! Stop touchin' me there! Stop! Help! This man's touchin' me! Help! No! Stop it! Stop touchin' me there!"

The stunned guard released his grip just as the door burst open behind him and two husky men in blue uniforms entered the washroom.

"You like playin' with boys, do ya!?" said one of the men as they each grabbed an arm and lifted him protesting past Dewey and Stevie to slam him into the far wall. "Let's see how you like playing with the big boys, eh?"

As the men beat the guard, Blue slid off the counter and signaled Stevie and Dewey to leave, and they did. They ran into the food court, raced down the mall, rushed into Sears, flew down the escalator, and charged out the glass doors of the entrance, where they stopped to catch their breath.

"That was damn incredible! Did yas see 'em slam 'im face first in the wall? Unbelievable! They came right in and started wailing on him! Let's see that guy tries ta push us around again! See, Dwight, that's the power of bein' a kid."

Dewey didn't understand what had happened, but it got them out of trouble, so from his perspective at that moment, the outcome was positive.

"I got my shit back too!" Blue said as he held up the bag holding the lighter. "Hey, does ya knows ya have dick on yer hands! Yas didn't wash it off!" Blue laughed, and when Steve smiled and put up his palm to high-five, he instinctively slapped it and was immediately disgusted. "Funny. Really, really funny. Now I got yer dick on my hand."

Then, after Blue winked at Stevie, they both rubbed their hands on Dewey's jacket, his hair, and his face.

"Damn it to hell, you guys!"

Stopping his assault on Dewey, Blue said, "Damn it ta hell? That's a new one for ya."

"My dad used to say it."

With Stevie whispering in his ear, Blue said, "Oh, right. We've gots ta go ups and outs the other side. Okay, everyone with dick on their hands... and face, follow me and walk normal like, takin' are time like."

Casually making their way up to the next level of Sears, they exited through a set of revolving doors to stand on a nine-foot-wide sidewalk at the edge of what was a huge parking lot with several taxis lined up to their right and several buses parked further down to their left. "Hey, look at that," Blue said, causing Dewey and Stevie to look to the right where an ambulance with its lights flashing was driving toward a police car that had two handcuffed men in blue uniforms being forced into the back. "That was fast. Now I know whys the cops are always parked by malls."

After one of the men looked over toward the boys and said something to the police officers, Blue said, "Come on! The twenty just got 'ere. Talk about great timin'!"

Blue ran down the sidewalk, entered the gray and blue bus, and told the driver he was paying for three, and after he counted out the change and dropped it into the metal box beside the driver, the bus pulled out, and Dewey and Stevie followed him to a row of four seats at the back.

On the bus ride back to Autumn Drive, Blue and Stevie cheerfully talked about what had happened. Blue said something. Stevie whispered in his ear. Blue said something else, and the cycle repeated itself several times with laughter occasionally thrown in.

While his friends talked and laughed, Dewey quietly reflected on the incident and found himself questioning Blue's action. Was it right what happened to the three men? Did one deserve to get so beaten that they had to call an ambulance? Should Blue have tricked the two men into rescuing them, only to have them arrested and maybe go to jail? It seemed much too selfish to be right. What's the worse the security guard would've done to them? Would he have called the police, called their parents, or banned them from the mall, just as they banned Blue from the store? Physically, he probably wouldn't have done anything more to them than what little he had done to Blue, and being banned from the mall didn't seem like such a big deal when there were more malls around. And if the guard had called the police or his mom, the worse that would happen, he guessed, was a long grounding. Then deciding that he would've gladly taken a grounding to avoid the man being hurt and the two being arrested, he blurted out, "What you... what we did was wrong! We got those men in a lot of trouble! We shouldn't have done that!"

Stunned by their friend's scolding, Blue and Stevie glanced at each other before staring down at their laps and saying nothing more during the rest of the bus ride.

That Sunday after Mother's Day and after an evening of Pong and Pizza, when Dewey surprised Avriel by exclaiming, "Shit!" twice during the game, Avriel dropped Dewey off at home and before leaving, watched the boy exchange a few words with Art at the steps before entering the building.

"Hi, Mom. I'm home. Art told me he's carving a dragon and using a bigger piece of wood too."

Stopping where he was, Dewey was surprised to find Frank sitting on the sofa next to his mother. Each was holding a glass of red wine, and there was an empty wine bottle on the coffee table.

"Hi, Honey! François and I were just talking about you. He was saying how you, Stevie, and Blue would make a great three musketeers."

Cautiously, sitting down on the other side of his unusually cheerful mother, he asked, "What's a musketeer?"

"They were swordsmen in France, the protectors of the King — heroes," Frank said with more of a French accent than usual.

"Cool. Where's Blue?"

"He's outside with Stevie," Lisa said, and as if reading her son's mind, she added, "It's too late to go out. It's almost seven and a school night. You'll be coming in again in a few minutes and Stevie should be going home about now, too."

"Okay, can I watch TV?"

"Oh, Honey, Frank and I are talking. Could you read or play in your room?"

"Okay," Dewey said with obvious disappointment.

Dewey spent the next hour and a half reading *The Hobbit* before his mother came in to tell him it was bedtime, and after he changed into his pajamas, washed his face, brushed his teeth, and met the two in the living room, he kissed his mother goodnight and shook Frank's hand and wished him a good night too.

In the early hours of the morning, he woke up with a dry mouth and got out of bed to walk half-awake and barefoot to the kitchen. Rinsing one of the wine glasses in the sink, he filled it with water, and after quenching his thirst, he turned to leave the kitchen and noticed a man's pair of shoes next to the door, which made no sense to him. Walking down the hall, he opened the door of his mother's room and tried to make sense of what he was seeing there too. With the sheets pulled up to his armpits, Frank was asleep on his back next to his mother, who was sleeping on her side with her arm resting on his chest. As Dewey stood staring at the couple, tears ran down his cheeks. It could've been a minute or ten minutes, he would never know, but eventually, he left the bedroom and closed the door.

As Dewey wiped his eyes with the sleeves of his pajamas, Blue's words flashed through his mind: *Dwight'll have another dad in no time*. Then anger engulfed him, one so strong and unfamiliar that it made his thin arms shake.

After struggling to unlock his apartment door with his shaking hand, he ran down the hall to Blue's door. He wanted to kick it in. He needed to kick it in, so he kicked it hard with the ball of his foot, making much less noise than he wanted to make and causing a sharp pain in his foot. *Dwight'll have another dad in no time*. He kicked the door again to the same effect, and then, ignoring the pain, he kicked it again and again and again.

When the door opened, a confused Blue in his tighty-whities said, "Man, the door's unlocked. What ya doin'?"

Dewey pushed him into the kitchen. "IT'S YOUR FAULT! IT'S ALL YOUR FAULT!"

"What is? What the hell are ya talkin' about?" Blue asked, pushing Dewey out of the kitchen.

"YOUR DAD, MY MOM! THEY'RE TOGETHER! TOGETHER, RIGHT NOW!"

"Calm down and close the door."

With Dewey standing there covered in anger, Blue pushed him aside, closed the door, and walked toward the living room.

He planned this! He knew what was going to happen!

"Again, what's the—"

With a loud cry, Dewey lunged at him and both fell to the floor. Kneeling over his chest, Dewey slapped him several times before Blue pushed him off, reversed positions, and used his knees to hold down his arms.

"Man, what the hell are ya doin'?"

"IT'S ALL YOUR FAULT! YOU KNEW THIS WOULD HAPPEN! YOU KNEW IT ALL ALONG!"

"My dad's with yer mom?"

"YES! IT'S ALL YOUR FAULT!"

Blue got off Dewey. "Just a sec, champ."

Walking to his father's bedroom, he looked in and returned to Dewey still on the floor. "Get up," he said as he bent down and held out his hand, and after Dewey reluctantly took it and he pulled him to his feet, Blue touched his lip and looked at the bit of blood on his finger. "Ya know, ya have ta makes a fist when ya hits someone. That practicin' open-handed boxin' is just so yas don't hurts each other." With Dewey standing there with anger still in his eyes, he pointed to the sofa. "Sit down. Sit down... *please*," and when his friend reluctantly followed him to the sofa, Blue said, "Ya know, adults needs affection. They needs sex. Ya gets it, right?"

"Sex? You mean making babies?"

"Or... when they pretends ta make babies, most pretends. Look, if it wasn't Frank, it could be some other guy, some creep. And ya knows what? I don't sees anythin' wrong with 'em together. Look, ya know Frank's cool. He doesn't date much and he don't sex around."

"You said I would have another dad! I don't want another dad!"

Finding his impatience difficult to control, Blue said, "They're just havin' sex! Frank's not goin' ta be yer father! They're just havin' sex! That's why boyfriends and girlfriends exist!" Releasing a huff, he added, "Besides, would it be so bad if 'e was yer dad too? We'd be brothers, step-brothers, but still brothers."

Blue is right. Shit! Christ! Shit! Blue is right!

The pressure again grew behind Dewey's eyes. He was no longer angry. Instead, he felt bad for his father possibly being replaced while not being able to do anything about it, and he felt bad for accusing and attacking Blue. Then, spotting the clock on the living room wall and reminded of how late it was, he stood up and said, "You're right... I'm... I'm sorry. You might want to put a Band-Aid on your lip."

As Blue followed Dewey to the door, he said, "Dwight, we shouldn't mention we knows about 'em. We should let 'em tells us. Besides, they might decides they're better at just bein' friends... or enemies."

Dewey didn't understand what Blue meant with the last part and said only, "Okay," and left.

He had timed it well. He only started crying as he walked to his apartment.

In the morning, Frank would be gone before Dewey woke, and as per Blue, he wouldn't say anything to his mother regarding the night before, leaving her to wonder why he was so grumpy during both breakfast and their morning walk to school.

Later that morning, her curiosity would be replaced by shock and grief.

CHAPTER 9
Unadulterated Evil

Sunday evening was the week's peak time for children playing outside. With the school week starting the next day and little on regular television to keep them in front of it, most joined their friends outside. That was the only problem with Sunday evenings: the children were together. It would be difficult to find one alone, and because of that, he normally didn't bother 'hunting' on Sunday evenings.

Over the last three weeks, he had been familiarizing himself with the townhouses along Carson Street. With the area surrounded by forest, he felt certain it had potential. He just had to find the right spot, which he expected was somewhere behind the forest line surrounding the blocks of townhouses.

Then one evening while smoking behind the steering wheel of his car parked on the first street off of Carson, he was losing hope of finding the spot when he noticed a teenage boy coming out from a break between the townhouses. Several minutes later, a younger child appeared, and a few minutes after that, a group of four boys. Curious, he left the security of his car's tinted windows to see where they were coming from, and finding a well-worn path of dirt and rock, he followed it almost to its end, where it sloped steeply down toward Herring

Cove Road.

It only occurred to him then that a forest's path could function as a selection line. All he had to do was wait for a single child to make its way along it, and if the child were suitable, he would just take him. It could never be easier than that.

Excited by his revelation, he spent some time familiarizing himself with the area on each side of the path, and just before the setting sun forced him to leave, he found what he considered the perfect killing ground.

That next Sunday evening, waiting just off the path in the hope of finding a child alone, he wiped the perspiration from his brow, dried his hands on his jacket, and opened it. It was chilly, but not chilly enough to cool his excitement. A breeze would've been appreciated, but the trees blocked any chance of that, much like it seemed to block the sounds. Except for the repeated harsh clicking of a squirrel protesting his presence, there wasn't a bird chirping, the leaves weren't rustling, and hardly a sound could be heard coming from the children yelling among the townhouses a few minutes away, and that meant from where he was, hardly a sound could be heard at the townhouses, further exciting him.

Needing to calm down, he reached into his jacket pocket and took out a pack of Export 'A' cigarettes. Placing one between his dry lips, he pulled out a book of matches, tore one off, swiped it against the book's rough strip, and with a long drag, the end of the cigarette grew bright red. Holding the smoke in his lungs for several seconds, its chemicals relaxed him slightly. Then slowly releasing it through his nose, he thought it odd that even though he had turned up the game by prolonging the kills, it was his first, the simplest and the quickest, that had given him the most intense rush followed by an overwhelming feeling in the pit of his stomach. A feeling much like he had experienced as a youth when he had jumped from a cliff high above the cold lake. Since his first kill, that feeling in his stomach had weakened dramatically, just as it did when, after several jumps into the water, it became almost nonexistent.

He would always remember his first. The rush had started even before he had grabbed the child and it reached its peak as he saw for the first time a pair of eyes go from surprise to terror. It had even maintained its intensity while the body twisted about wildly for air until the child was unconscious and then dead. He thought the powerful rush was a combination of both the kill and the fear of being caught during the moment, and since that fear no longer existed, maybe the rush could never be as strong.

Dropping the cigarette, he crushed it with his sneaker, and then hearing voices, he crouched down as they got louder. Seconds later, two teens passed where he was hiding. After waiting a minute, he returned to the path and followed it to where it started its drop and where he could easily look down onto Herring Cove Road.

Hiding among the trees, he watched as small groups of teens struggled up it to pass him, unsuspecting, and after forty minutes and growing disappointed, he was considering giving up for the night when a small blond heading toward the bottom of the path caught his attention. He thought he might know him, and as the child got closer, he did know him, making it a new experience and a good chance he'll finally experience the rush again.

After waiting to make sure the boy was coming his way and with his heart pounding hard with the excitement of his good fortune, he headed up the path, and at about its midway point, he took in several large breaths to calm down while waiting for the small footsteps to approach. When he heard them, he called out, "Sampson! Here, boy! Come here, boy!" And in seconds, he and the child were face to face. "Hey! Great, it's you! I was walkin' my girlfriend's dog and mades the damn mistake of not holdin' the leash tight enough. He just took off after a squirrel, leash and all!"

With a confused look on his face, the boy glanced back in the direction of where he had come, and then looking curiously at the familiar man standing in front of him, he pointed his index finger at him and then shook his thumb over his shoulder as if to ask, "Didn't I just see you back there?"

"Yeah, yeah, I'll explain later. Right now, I've gotta finds the dog. Come on. Ya'll be doin' me a solid if ya helps. If I don't finds the dog, I'm dead. Really, she's gots 'er a serious temper."

The child put his hand out. "Fifty cents."

Taken aback by the child's words, he said, "What? Jesus Christ! We're wastin' time! It'll be dark soon!"

With the boy's hand still out, he pulled his wallet from his back pocket and took out a two-dollar bill. "Keep the change."

Tucking the money into his back pocket, the boy entered the woods, yelling, "SAMPSON!"

They only walked a short way before they came to the square wall of stones, where the boy was confused by the plastic grocery bag lying in the middle of the familiar graveyard and the several strips of dark-green duct tape hanging from a small slanted gravestone, and before he could make sense of what he was seeing, his thin arms were locked, his mouth was covered by a hand and he was lifted over the wall, and as he attempted several muffled screams, the hand over his mouth was replaced by a strip of duct tape.

Then on his back in the center of the square with his arms and ankles duct-taped together, the child did something none of those in the past had done. He did nothing. He didn't struggle, didn't cry, and didn't make a sound. He just stared up at the man kneeling beside him and watched as his jacket was opened and his T-shirt was pulled up to his armpits, revealing his small chest.

"Yup, I'm that guy everyone's talkin' abouts. Surprise! And after today, there'll be a lot more talkin'. No tryin' ta hide the bodies anymore, eh?" Pulling out a pocketknife and then pulling out its blade, he could feel the rush building. "Tonight, we're gonna play a different sorta game. One thats... thats ya've already lost."

CHAPTER 10
Goodbye

Mounted discreetly into the ceiling, the speakers filled the large room with soft organ music. Covering the walls from floor to ceiling was a wallpaper of large blood-red flowers on a white background with a few brown and green flowers scattered among them, which from a distance were unrecognizable and appeared as a dark mix of morbid colors. From the ceiling hung two rows of three conservative chandeliers, illuminating the room and causing everything in it to cast multiple shadows of various degrees. Behind the small dark-stained casket at the front of the room hung several white curtains, and a dozen feet in front of it were rows of chairs running two-thirds of the room's length and stopping ten feet from the opened double doors at the back. And scattered throughout the room were several small wooden tables, each containing a ceramic or glass vase of white roses.

The mourners, an almost even mix of White and Black, wore either a blank expression or one of grief. While some quietly sat on the chairs, others mingled, whispering and throwing out the occasional moan.

Wearing a new black suit, Blue stood beside the opened top half of the casket looking at the face of the gray-suited child within, the room's only peaceful face that made him question if there was any truth to the awful rumors of how he had died. Looking at the framed photo resting on the closed lower half of the casket, the full-teeth mischievous smile and the sparkling devil-may-care eyes, which he was used to, made him wish his friend would sit up, laugh and then whisper, "Ya fells fer it so easy!" It was all just a big joke, perhaps overkill, but certainly in poor taste.

As he was wiping an eye, a hand gently touching his shoulder brought him back to reality, and he looked to the side to see Mr. Delaney with what was left of his remaining gray hair greased back and the two buttons of his suit jacket straining to keep it closed. Next to the man, in a black dress and her hair in a bun, Mrs. Delaney stood nodding as her husband whispered to him, but with his whisper mixing in with the low buzz from the many others in the room, Blue couldn't make out what was said and responded with only a nod before turning back to look at Stevie.

With the Delaneys gone, he touched his friend's cheek, and startled by its cold feel, he jerked his hand away, examined the bit of powder on it, and wiped it against his black suit pants.

Behind Blue, Mrs. Kelly sat in the first row of chairs, and to her right, from the shortest to tallest, her three dark-haired boys sat up stiffly. In front of her and her sons, a semi-circle of mourners stood giving their condolences, and as they left, others immediately took their place. The heartbroken mother would've stood to be courteous, but earlier she had collapsed and would most likely do it again.

Two rows behind Stevie's mother and looking at everything in front of her but seeing nothing, Lisa sat holding Avriel and Dewey's hands, intermittently releasing one or the other's to wipe her tears with the tissue lying on her lap.

Feeling someone staring at him, Avriel looked back to see

Mr. Parker standing by the double doors, and excusing himself, he stood up and slowly made his way to the back, where both left in the direction of the funeral director's office.

Sitting in his little world of grief, Dewey was pulled out of it by a hand on his shoulder, and after each nodded to the other, Blue sat down next to him, loosened his black tie, released the button on his collar, and joined the boy in staring ahead as if looking at an invisible speaker only they could see giving a silent speech only they could hear.

There was no speaker at the funeral, no priest or minister giving a sermon, and no eulogies. It was a room of silent remembrance, whispered condolences, and subtle comments registering the shock of the recent event.

"Did yas eat?" Blue whispered.

Dewey shook his head

"Ya wanna?"

Nodding his head, Dewey was thankful to have an interruption and grateful to have Blue finally talk to him. It had been three days since they had seen each other.

While sitting and holding his mother's hand, he had been trying to make sense of what had happened to Stevie. There were so many things he wanted to ask his mother and Avriel, but wasn't sure when it would be the right time. He had learned three days before, after he had asked her how it happened, that his questions brought her tears, and when he asked Avriel the same question, it surprised him to see the old man's eyes water and he couldn't understand his mumbling through his accent. Nothing made sense to the boy. For the last three days, every adult around him whispered: his mother to Avriel, Avriel to his mother, and even Frank when he dropped by to briefly whisper to his mother. Even the police were whispering when they came asking questions. Dewey had thought they were doing it for his benefit until he showed up at the funeral and everybody there was doing it as well.

Noticing Blue, Lisa offered a sympathetic look and released her son's hand to reach over and squeeze his. "Hi, Blue," she whispered.

"Hello, Mrs. Dixon. Is it okay if Dwight joins me for a sandwich at the food table?"

Lisa forced a smile and a nod before again facing forward.

Dewey followed Blue to a clothed table by the entrance, where standing by it and talking to a man in jeans and a dress shirt was a detective he immediately recognized from the previous fall, when Avriel discovered a child's body. As he and Blue each took a paper plate and selected from the assortment of finger sandwiches and pastries, Dewey tried to eavesdrop on what the detective was saying. He had a hard time making out their whispers, but it seemed like the detective was asking for information. Then, after giving his card to the man, the detective moved on to a small, heavyset woman whose voice filled the room as she berated him for allowing another murder, smacked his arm, and then walked away in disgust.

With his plate filled to satisfaction, Blue said, "Let's get outta 'ere."

Nodding his head before squeezing a small pastry into his mouth, Dewey followed him out of the room, down a hall, and through a set of open doors where both had to squint while their eyes painfully adjusted to the mid-afternoon rays. As both sat to the side of the wide wooden steps, Blue whispered, "It's time we starts wearin' sunglasses," and placed a small pastry in his mouth.

"Yup," Dewey whispered back.

"Pretty nice day for a funeral," Blue said past the pastry.

"I guess," Dewey said before taking a bite of an egg sandwich and appreciating that there was no crust.

Blue swallowed what was in his mouth. "I feel so spacey, almost drunk... high as a kite. I haven't slept good since it happened. My head won't turn off," he said as he rubbed his face with his palms. "Hey, I'm sorry about not bein' around the last few nights. Me and Frank were with Stevie's mom most of the time, and when I was home, I needed ta be alone."

"It's okay," Dewey said.

But it wasn't okay. Several times over the past three evenings, believing Frank had gone to work and expecting Blue to be home, Dewey had knocked on their door but got no response. From outside the building, he had seen the apartment lights on, and when he put his ear to their apartment door, he thought he heard noises inside, but after a few minutes of his knocks being ignored, he left with watery eyes, thinking Blue was still angry with him for his midnight attack.

"I'm sorry about getting mad at you. It wasn't right. Are we... are we still friends?" Dewey asked.

"What? Of course, we're still friends. Don't worry about it. I already forgots about 'er. It takes a lot more than that ta lose my respects fer ya. If anythin', I respects ya more because of it."

"Seriously?"

"Yeah, seriously. How are ya holdin' up?"

"I'm... I'm not sure. Mom and Av told me about Stevie after school Monday. Well, Av told me. Mom was crying in her room when we got home. It only sunk in today that he's gone... dead. I didn't... I couldn't believe he was. I don't know why, but I just couldn't. It just makes no sense. How could he be dead? We were just with him Sunday afternoon."

"Yeah, I hears ya. Like 'e hadn't gone through enough in 'is life ta have ta end up like this!" Realizing he was being loud, Blue checked himself and whispered, "Ya should've known 'im before the stutterin'. Ya know he didn't always stutter, right? He's hilarious. He can tells a joke like nobody else. And pranks, he loves pullin' pranks."

"Stutter? I didn't know he stuttered. I only know he was shy."

"Nah, he wasn't shy. He was never shy. Well... maybe abouts 'is stutterin'. He stutters big time. If 'e says more than three or four words, he stutters like, 'I'm goin' ta aunt Rach-ch-ch-ch-chel'sss t-t-t-to s-s-s-see...' It takes 'im forever ta finish a sentence. That's why 'e whispers all the times. Once 'e figured out 'e could whisper withouts stutterin', that's all 'e does... most of the time. He can sing withouts stutterin' too, but that'd be crazy, right?

"It's a new thing, maybe two years. It came on slowly like, after 'is... 'is asshole father left. He used ta beat him, beat 'im hard and call 'im names. He's a major asshole. Ya know, I asked Stevie hows 'e can take 'is father beatin'im. It's no big deal, he tells me. He got use ta it... it didn't hurts much after the first few times. His stutterin' gots a lot worser too after 'is uncle shot another one dead."

Dewey stopped eating, looked at Blue, and tried to whisper, but little came out of his partially filled mouth. Swallowing, he whispered again, "His father beat him, and his uncle killed another uncle? Seriously?"

"Yeah, makes ya think how goods ya got 'er, right? You know that triplex we passes behind to go ta the playground? A couple years back, his uncle, an alchy, lived there and—"

"What's an alchy?"

"An alcoholic... his uncle was an alcoholic, always drunk and all that. He was threatenin' ta hurt his wife... Mrs. Kelly's sister, so Mrs. Kelly's brother put a shotgun in a garbage bag and went ta the alchy's place. Stevie and I were hangin' outside it when 'e drives up and tells us ta leave... of course we didn't, but we should've. He went in the buildin' and then

BANG! Stevie lost two uncles, one died and the other wents ta prison. And after that, 'is stutterin' gots a whole lot worser."

"I... didn't know that. I didn't know any of that," Dewey said, looking out onto Herring Cove Road as pressure built up in his face and he tried to hold back his tears. "Is... is his dad here now?"

"No, he wouldn't dare show 'is face 'ere. And anyways, he hates Stevie. Don't ask me why 'cause I never gots it." Blue tossed a piece of sandwich onto the lawn for the birds. "This whole thing is crazy! I swear I'm going to find this freak myself! The cops ain't doin' nothin'!"

"It looks like the detective's trying to do something."

"What detective?"

"The man in the dark-gray suit. The one with the thin mustache giving people little pieces of paper. He was there after Av found the dead boy at the baseball field."

Blue stopped short of putting a quarter piece of tuna sandwich into his mouth. "He found Keith? Damn, it's a small world!"

"Huh?"

"Keith was a kid of Frank's friend. Frank and Tim played cards at his house sometimes. He was the first victim of the Kid Killer."

"The Kid Killer? The first?"

"Yeah. There were two kids killed... and Stevie makes three. Ya didn't know that?"

"Stevie was murdered?"

"Are ya kiddin' me? What the hell ya thinks 'e died from, a heart attack?"

Dewey cried. "I don't know! Damn it to hell! I don't know anything! No one tells me anything! Av told me the boy's uncle did it!"

Blue placed his arm around Dewey's shoulder again. "I'm

sorry man, I just figureds someone would've told ya. Hey, it's okay. Yeah, they thought 'is uncle did it... 'cause 'e didn't have an alibi. But it turns out 'e did. He was havin' sex with 'is sister-in-law and didn't want anyones ta know. So no one told ya they found Stevie at the graveyard?"

"No!" Dewey said, raising his eyebrows and voice before wiping his eyes on the sleeve of his suit jacket.

"Yeah, they found 'im all cut up, tortured. Sunday night his mom was visitin' her friend next door and thought 'e came home that night, but the next mornin' found out 'e didn't. The cops were already there when I showed up ta walk with 'im ta school. I told 'em where we hung out at... and... and that's where they found 'im.

"A lot a kids die around here. Three murdered... and last winter three others died too. Greg died usin' his brother's weight bench. Some girl died last winter buildin' a snow igloo... and another kid, some retarded kid, was hit by a car. That's six I knows of... in maybe a year."

Hearing nothing after the word *tortured*, Dewey asked, "Why'd he torture him?"

"I'm guessin' the Kid Killer's a pervert too."

"Is that like an introvert? I heard Mrs. Rosen... Av's wife say introverts are misunderstood."

With a dumbfounded look, Blue shook his head. "No. No, it's nothin' like that. It's a sex maniac. Some men likes men more than women, and some of those likes boys, and those are perverts."

"Seriously?"

"Yeah, some men are pretty messed up in the head. Ya always gots ta be careful arounds strange men. Hey, uh... has... has Mr. Rosen ever... ever touched ya... touched ya on the crotch?"

"On the crotch? No! Why would he do that?"

"That's it. That's exactly it. He wouldn't, but a pervert woulds."

"Oh... okay," Dewey said, not understanding what Blue was saying.

For a couple of minutes, the two ate in silence, until Blue said, "This is my first funeral. Normally they cremates 'em, and it's done with. They're only havin' this 'ere 'cause it's a *unanimous* donation. Hey, ya goin' ta the burial tomorrow?"

Dewey said nothing as he stared across the road, reflecting on all that Blue had said.

"Hey, ya goin' ta the burial tomorrow?" he asked again.

"Huh? I–I don't know. I only found out we were coming here this morning."

"Well, I'm goin' with Tim. Yer welcome ta tag along if ya wants."

"No. I mean... no thanks. If... if Av doesn't go, I won't either."

"Okay. Hey, I gots somethin' impor'ant ta tells ya, real impor'ant, but not 'ere. I'll tells ya tonight. Come over after supper, alright?"

Dewey nodded his head. "Sure, okay."

As the two watched a car drive into the funeral home's parking lot, Blue said, "Let's get back. I wanna leave before the teachers starts showin' up. It's weird seein'em outta school. Makes me feel kinda bad for givin'em a hard time."

Both stood up and brushed the butt of their suit pants before Blue took Dewey's empty plate and the two entered the building.

Inside the room of whispers, Blue left Dewey to join Frank, who was talking to the Delaneys at the front, and Dewey joined his mother and Avriel as they sat silent.

At home, after Lisa hugged Dewey and Avriel before

retiring to her bedroom, Avriel got out a partially built model jet and the two began working on it, and while they were examining the instructions to see how the next piece went on, Dewey asked Avriel if he thought Stevie was in heaven. Noticeably awkward by the question, Avriel thought for a few seconds and then told his small friend he was certain all children went to heaven. Dewey then asked if the killer would go to hell, and without giving it a second thought, Avriel said, "Yes." Dewey was satisfied with both answers.

**

It was a little after six when Dewey, in jeans and a solid gray T-shirt, showed up at Blue's apartment and was surprised to find his friend still in his suit pants and dress shirt.

"How's yer mom doin'?" Blue asked after greeting him at the door.

Inviting himself in, Dewey said, "She's really sad. Av says she needs time to deal with everything. She sleeps a lot. Av is sleeping over tonight. He's been sleeping on the sofa for two days now. You should hear him snore. Mom says she's surprised Mrs. Publicover hasn't complained yet."

"Come inta the kitchen," Blue said as he walked over to the short counter where Dewey joined him. "Mr. Rosen is pretty nice. I like 'im. He's pretty funny when 'e acts stupid, and not many people can acts stupid and be funny doin' it. Only smart ones can," Blue said before pulling out a drawer and taking out a steak knife. "Ever hear of blood brothers?"

"Nope."

"It's a ritual thing ta make two people better than friends. Like brothers that'll be there fer each other in good times and bad. They gots each other's backs forever and any promises or secrets between 'em stays between 'em forever. Ya can't choose yer real brother, but ya can choose yer blood brother."

"Oh, it's sort of like best buddies. Av and I are best

buddies. He says a person can have up to four at a time, boys or girls. He read it in a law book."

Blue stared at Dewey for a second. "Right... no, this is stronger than that... I think. Ya can only have one blood brother. Stevie is... was mine, and now that he's gone..." Blue took in a deep breath. "Now that he's gone, I wants ya ta be my blood brother. It seems even more fittin' seein' how we don't have no real brothers, right?"

With a wave of pride hitting him, Dewey asked, "What do we do?"

"We makes a cut in are finger, then we touches 'em together ta mix the bloods."

Dewey watched with apprehension as Blue pulled a lighter from his front pocket, flicked it, and for a second held its flame to the tip of the steak knife. When he put the lighter back in his pocket and examined the tip of the knife, Dewey instinctively took a step backward. "Relax. It only stings a bit," Blue reassured him, and then proving it, he poked the tip of his index finger and held it up to show the tiny drop of blood slowly growing bigger. "Okay, do it now before mine dries."

Blue handed the knife to Dewey, who closed his eyes, grimaced, and pushed the tip of the blade against the tip of his index finger. He tried, but he couldn't push it in. Then something hit the knife, causing it to poke his finger. "Damn it to hell!" Dewey yelled as he opened his eyes to see Blue's face covered with a smile so big that his top and bottom teeth were showing.

"What? It looked like ya needed some help there. Okay, let's mix the blood," Blue said, taking his little friend's finger, placing the tip of his against it, and holding it there. "With this blood, I make thee my blood brother fer life. Now ya says it."

"With this blood, I make... I make thee my blood brother for life."

"Cool. Now, we're officially blood brothers."

Turning on the cold water, Blue placed his finger under it, and after Dewey did the same, each dried their fingers with a dish towel and put on a small band-aid that Blue had earlier set aside.

"Okay, I tolds ya I hads somethin' impor'ant to tell ya. But first, what I'm goin' ta shows ya, ya gotta keep a secret forever... and I means forever. We never tells no one, understand?"

Dewey nodded with more apprehension than he had when he found out he was going to have to poke his finger.

"Okay, follow me."

Blue led Dewey to his bedroom, kicked the dirty clothes scattered on the floor toward the closet door, and sat down on the edge of his unmade bed.

Sitting down beside him, Dewey noticed two toy handguns at the foot of the bed. "Cool!" he said, picking up the dull black one with a longer barrel and realizing by its weight that it wasn't plastic but metal.

"They're the real thing, the real McCoys. Frank keeps 'em for protection."

"Protection from what?" Dewey asked, turning the gun over in his hands.

"They're for 'is work."

Dewey tore his eyes from the gun to look at Blue. "But he's at work now and the guns are here?"

"Not for the mall. Guns are only for the cops there. For his other work. I'll tells ya abouts that some other time. Okay... this is our first secret as blood brothers. Frank doesn't know I knows abouts 'em. They're not loaded. He keeps the bullets separate, but I knows where they are too," Blue said, reaching under his pillow and pulling out seven bullets. "I took some from the box yesterday. They're for the little shiny one there on the bed. What ya gots there is a World War Two Luger... the Germans used 'em."

"A German? Seriously? That is too cool! Scary... but cool!"

After Blue stuffed the bullets into his pocket, he took the gun from Dewey and pulled back on the top, forcing a section on the top's back end to pop up into a triangle and a bullet to pop out.

"Shit. I didn't think it was loaded. Uh... that's... that's what yas does ta load the first bullet... or remove it. It takes a metal thing that holds the bullets in the handle. Frank keeps it with the bullets."

Blue passed the Luger back to Dewey, and as he picked up the smaller shiny revolver, Dewey pointed the Luger at the wall and pretended to pull the trigger. "Bang... bang," he said and then wondered if Avriel had a gun, but then figured that since he had kept nothing from the war, not even his medals, he would never have kept a gun.

"Now this little one here's the coolest. Its box says it's a Colt Agent. Even the name's cool, right?"

With Blue holding it out to him, Dewey set the Luger on the bed, examined the revolver, and decided the Luger was much cooler, if only because of its history.

"Pull the pin in front there and that round thing there'll come out."

Dewey pulled the ejector rod forward and watched the cylinder dropped out to the side. Spinning it, he saw that its five slots were empty, and pushed it back into place. Pulling the rod again, the cylinder dropped out again, and like he had seen people do on television, with a quick twist of his wrist, he flicked the revolver and snapped the cylinder back in place.

"It's small, right? Feel how it fits in yer hand. It's like it's made for us, right?"

"Yup, it's perfect," Dewey nodded.

With it almost comfortable in his small hand, Dewey pointed the gun at the wall and pulled back the hammer, producing a double click, and then pulling the trigger slightly, the hammer snapped down. Pulling the trigger again, it took more effort as it lifted the hammer before slamming it down.

Blue left the room to return seconds later wearing his spring jacket. Taking the gun from Dewey, he placed it in the pocket of his jacket. "Can ya tell it's there?"

"Not really. I can tell something is there, but I can't tell it's the gun."

"That's what I figured too."

Handing it back to Dewey, Blue took off his jacket, laid it over a pillow, and sat down on the bed next to his friend, who continued playing with the revolver.

"Okay, the big news is I gots a plan ta catch Stevie's killer."

Dewey released the cylinder and with a flick of his wrist, snapped it back into place. He was going to do it again when Blue grabbed the revolver from him and laid it down behind him, causing Dewey to place his hands awkwardly on his lap.

"I gots a plan ta catch the killer, but I need yer help. It's really simple. Ya'll act as the bait, and I'll hide and watch. When the guy goes ta grabs ya, I comes out and shoots 'im dead."

Having a hard time believing what he was hearing, Dewey paused before asking, "Uh... Uh, but... but why can't you be the bait and I come out and shoot him?"

"Because he likes 'em small. Stevie's yer size and Keith was yer size. I'd do it alls on my own if I coulds, but the freak likes 'em small. And I'm not sure ya'd have it in ya ta shoots when ya had ta."

Having to fight the feeling of being insulted about his size,

Dewey thought about what Blue had said, decided he was more right than wrong, and asked, "Okay, when do we start?"

Blue smiled and said with some excitement, "Cool! He kills abouts every few months maybe, so we should waits about two or three weeks and then start. If we starts too early, it might give are plan away." Then Blue paused as a thought occurred to him. "Hey, ya don't have ta do this because we're blood brothers, ya know. Being a blood brother doesn't mean ya gots ta do everythin' yer blood brother wants. Are ya sure yer cool with it?"

Dewey wasn't, but said, "Yup, but we have to do it before it gets dark. Mom always wants me home before it's dark."

"Right, I know, and that's okay, 'cause the killer prob'ly wants ta kill ya before it gets dark too."

Dewey's apprehension wasn't going away, so he tried to change the subject. "Okay, but... but what do we do before then, before we start using me as... as bait?"

"Nothin'... I mean, we do whats we always do... but withouts... without Stevie."

"Right," Dewey nodded, and then, with neither knowing what to say, both boys sat quietly for a few seconds.

"Hey, when ya goin' back ta school?"

"Tomorrow. Mom wants me to get all the stuff I'm behind on and catch up on the weekend. You?"

"Monday," Blue said as he grabbed the two guns and leaned down to slide them beneath the bed. Sitting back up, he yawned, causing Dewey to do the same. "Okay, so we've got a couple weeks to talk more abouts the plan and I'll have to starts practicin' shooting, but now I have ta try ta sleep. I haven't slept a wink since they found 'im."

Taking the hint, Dewey stood up. "Okay. If I get my homework all done, I'll talk to you on the weekend. If not, then Monday night for sure. I don't think this Saturday will be movie night," he said, and then a thought jumped into his head. "Hey, do you think they would give us a medal for catching the killer?"

"Sure... sure they might," Blue said with a smile as he stood up and led Dewey to the apartment door.

"Goodnight, big blood brother," Dewey said, smiling and waving behind him as he headed down the hall toward his apartment.

"Goodnight, little blood brother."

Blue closed the door and returned to his bed, reminding himself to do the laundry the next day. Moving his spring jacket from the pillow, he laid himself down on the bed to stare up at the ceiling. He didn't expect to sleep that night. There were too many repeated thoughts trespassing through his head from every direction. He couldn't believe Stevie was gone, couldn't believe there would be no more whispering in his ear, and couldn't help but think about what his friend must have gone through in the last minutes of his life — all because he didn't walk him home. His best friend was gone because he was careless and lazy. Then he did as he did each night since Monday: he got angry at himself for assuming the killings would never come so close to his world.

For the umpteenth time, Blue made a mental list of suspects. Could Tim be a suspect? He was strange, but that strange? Art? No, Art was on the steps carving away until the sun went down that night. Blue had seen him from his bedroom window. There was Jeff upstairs, whom Blue would visit occasionally to peruse his collection of Playboy magazines. No, Jeff was too into girls to be a suspect. Mr. Delany? No, he wouldn't have the energy. Mumphy? Mumphy certainly could've done it if he hadn't been working in the store that night. Whoever it is, they couldn't appear creepy, otherwise he never could've gotten close to Stevie without him being suspicious and guarded, and that ruled out the two brothers and the alcoholic carpenter living on his floor.

Eventually, Blue fell asleep only to wake up a few minutes later from a nightmare. He poured himself a glass of milk and watched television for a couple of hours before falling asleep again, only to wake up soon after from yet another nightmare. Around four in the morning, he decided to let alcohol put him to sleep, and after four beers he was drunk, but by eight in the morning, after several moments of breaking down and crying, he was sober, tired, and with a headache.

Insomnia wasn't new to Blue. He had gone through it when his mother had left without a goodbye. There wasn't even a note that afternoon when he returned from school to a lonely apartment, and there wasn't even a letter afterward. His mother had disappeared, and he only found out later from Frank that she had left with Pat, Frank's best friend, and was probably in New Brunswick.

Back then, Blue handled his insomnia differently. Then, at eight years old, he tossed and turned himself to sleep. Not the sporadic tossing and turning one might do throughout the night, but a continuous rolling from his back to his side and onto his back again, all the while moaning as he did it, eventually tiring himself out and falling asleep. He did that for almost a year before he could fall asleep without having to first physically burn off any stress.

**

Dewey went to bed with mixed emotions: he was grieving the loss of his blond-haired best buddy, was happy to be Blue's blood brother, and was worrying about Blue's plan. He only fell asleep after he reduced the emotions down to two, convincing himself not to worry about the plan since it was weeks away.

Sometime later, Avriel's snoring from the living room

woke Dewey, who then cycled through the same emotions he had when he went to bed, but with the addition of one more: he found it comforting to hear his best buddy snoring.

CHAPTER 11
Tim

After loosening his unfamiliar and uncomfortable tie, Tim reached up and lowered his and then Blue's sun visor. "I don't know why," he said, "but funerals make me feel... I don't know, almost horny."

Blue rolled his eyes. "Man, you can be so damn weird!"

Tim laughed. "That's true. Hey, I just realized why this 'ere feels different. We ain't often alone together, eh?"

"Nope," Blue said, leaning back into his seat and closing his eyes.

"So tell me somethin' abouts ya I don't knows. There's gotta be lots."

Keeping his eyes closed and wishing Tim would be as quiet coming from the burial as he was going to it, Blue said, "Not in the mood ta talk, man. Haven't slept in a while. My brain's dead."

"Okay... I gets that. Yeah, me too," Tim nodded before reaching out and turning the knob of the car's radio, which came on with a crackle before playing a rock song.

Neither spoke for several minutes until reaching the Armdale Rotary, where Tim made the counter-clockwise route around it to take Herring Cove Road. "It's hard to believe 'e's gone, eh?"

Pretending to be asleep, Blue didn't answer.

"It's hard to believe Stevie's gone, eh?" Tim repeated louder.

"Uh... yeah," Blue replied, keeping his eyes closed.

"Nice graveyard, eh?"

"Yeah."

"Pretty good burial too."

"As good as any... I guess. It's my first."

"Stevie's makes my third. We were close, ya know."

Blue said nothing. His mind was on his father. He felt bad that Frank had to trade two shifts that week, forcing him to work thirty-six hours straight and then another shift on Sunday night, but then Blue reminded himself that there were plenty of opportunities for naps during the night shifts.

Tim said louder, "Yeah, we were real close."

"Huh? Okay," Blue said, paying little attention to Tim as the sun's rays enhanced by the windshield were baking him in his black suit jacket while taunting him with sleep.

"We'd hang out together, ya know."

"Yeah, I know," Blue lied, hoping the man would shut up.

"So he told ya, eh?"

"Sure, yeah... he told me," Blue lied again.

"Cool. And ya weren't jealous?"

"Nah."

"Did he tell ya what we does?"

"Sure... yeah, sure," Blue lied yet again.

Tim slowed the car as he came up to the set of lights at the Cowie Hill subdivision, a hill of townhouses, and with the car stopped, he used his jacket sleeve to wipe the film of sweat from his forehead. "Yeah? And ya were cool with it?"

"Yeah, whatever."

"So, ya were cool with it? That's good. That's really good," Tim smiled, placing his hand on Blue's knee and squeezing it, causing the little man's eyes to snap open.

It wasn't the first time a man had tried to touch him, but was Tim's touch that sort of touch? Considering Tim's weird sense of humor, Blue wasn't sure.

"So, ya were cool with it! That's good, really, really good."

Blue tried to sound nonchalant. "Why... why wouldn't I be?"

"Yeah, right, why not? We guys have needs, eh?"

"Sure... sure."

"Would ya likes us ta be close too?"

As Tim's hand moved up his thigh, Blue tried to relax. He tried to pretend he didn't notice the touch. The touch that Mr. Bentley on the third floor of his building had once attempted. Old Mr. Bentley enjoyed watching wrestling, and after several conversations with Blue about it, he took him to the Halifax Forum to see the boy's favorite wrestler, Leaping Lenny. It was after they had arrived back at Mr. Bentley's apartment that the old man, standing behind Blue, reached around and grabbed Blue's crotch. Instinctively, Blue shot his elbow back, slamming it into the old man's groin, causing him to grunt and drop to the floor. Turning around to face him, Blue's shock was replaced by anger and he warned him that if he saw him with another child, "I'll tell Frank abouts what ya just did, and he'll do worser things than the police ever can!"

Blue never saw Mr. Bentley with another boy, but then soon after that, the man moved out of the building.

Then sweating more from the situation than from the sun, Blue found it difficult to accept Tim was a pervert, a sex maniac, or the term Frank had used several times earlier that week to describe the killer, a pedophile. He had never seen a sign of anything except the man's general weirdness, but there he was sitting beside him revealing his warped sexual preference.

Questions flew through Blue's mind. Could Tim be so desperate to find a new boy that it made him show his true self so impulsively and carelessly? Why would Tim try making a move on him? He wasn't passive. Tim didn't intimidate him. Did he give off the wrong vibe, the vibe that he liked men, liked men the way Tim liked boys? Why would Tim think he wouldn't see the connection between him molesting Stevie and him murdering Stevie? Did Tim think he was that stupid?

Blue had a strong urge to strike out, and he was only able to control himself by knowing that striking out at that moment wasn't the way to handle it. Tim was driving, was much stronger, and he wasn't sure how Tim would respond. Would he cower and apologize, become violent, or would he play it cool only to do something extreme when he stopped the car? Blue decided it was best to go along with the pervert until he could decide how to deal with him. He would strike out only when the time was right and when Tim wouldn't be able to strike back.

He needed air. He rolled his window down, set his seat in the upright position, and tried to control his growing anger.

"Would ya like us ta be close too?" Tim repeated.

"Sure... sure. Where... where'd we be close?" Blue asked as he looked straight ahead, avoiding looking at Tim out of fear he would impulsively strike the man.

"In the car. It's good for me. We can park somewheres more private."

"Nah, that's not... not very... very comfortable."

"Okay, how abouts yer place? Frank's at work. We'd have the place all ta us."

When the lights changed, Tim removed his hand from Blue's thigh and hit the gas hard, causing the wheels to squeal.

"Nah, I don't like that."

"Sure... okay... whatever ya want. How about the woods? Sometimes, me and Stevie plays in the woods. Why not the woods at the end a yer street? We have ta be discreet, so maybe one of us goes in before the other."

"Okay, ya goes in first and I'll change and meets ya there. I guess ya just go straight in, and... and I'll goes straight in ta meets ya."

"Cool. That's my Little Boy Blue always havin' a plan. Yer not so little anymore, though, eh?" Tim said through his heavy breathing. "Ya know I like ya, eh? Always have. Not sure why I waited so long ta tell ya."

Ya waited because ya already hads a boy toy, ya perv!

"I like ya too, Tim. I'm glad ya finally told me. It tooks ya long enough."

For the rest of the drive to Blue's apartment, neither spoke. Tim thought excitedly about what they would do, and Blue thought nervously about what he would do.

They parked in Frank's spot at the front of the building and when they got out, Tim whispered, "Okay... so I'll see ya in what, ten minutes?"

"Ten," Blue nodded awkwardly before leaving Tim to open the trunk, pull out an old dirt-stained sheet, and walk toward the woods at the end of the gravel road.

Having changed quickly, Blue sat on his bed in Jeans, a T-shirt, and a spring jacket and let out a loud primal yell, releasing some of the anger he had been struggling to control. Trying to control his racing heart, he had to remind himself not to get too emotional and not to get too excited. He didn't want to act impulsively. Then taking a deep breath, he left the apartment.

He entered the woods with his mind racing along with his heart. It was all just too easy, or it seemed to be. Tim wasn't a smart man, but how could he be so stupid to reveal himself so soon? Then Blue told himself it was no use trying to make sense of the pervert's reasoning. He should focus on what was to come. When he meets up with Tim, how should he approach the situation? Should he fly into him right away? Should he coax a confession out slowly, making Tim confide in him some more, just as he had done in the car? Maybe he should just go back home and call the police. But he couldn't just call them. He would have to call Frank first and explain everything, and he couldn't do that. He expected Frank would lose it and would want to handle it on his own, and the delay with him showing up in the woods was sure to give Tim a heads-up that his game was over and a head start on getting out of the city.

Blue tried to calm down by singing a song in his head. The first one to come to mind was *That's The Way (I Like It)* by KC and Sunshine Band, but that seemed to almost keep pace with his heart, so he changed it to another popular song at the time: *Bohemian Rhapsody* by the group Queen.

Before Blue realized it, he had come upon Tim leaning up against a tree anxiously tapping his hand against his thigh, and he was content that the freak was excited. It would make him less guarded and less prepared to lie when questioned.

"Hey there. Is this okay?" Tim asked, pointing to an area where he had spread out the dirt-stained bedsheet over a bed of pine needles blanketing the dirt and rock beneath. It was a small spot, a tight and confined space with three of its corners marked off with large pine trees.

"Sure, as good as any," Blue said as calmly as he could.

"Great. Let's get a little more comfortable."

Blue watched Tim take off his necktie, shove it in his pocket, unbutton the two top buttons of his shirt, and then sit down on the sheet. Patting the spot next to him, he said, "Okay, come here. I wanna unwraps ya."

With hands in his jacket pockets, Blue said, "So... so how longs ya been *playin'* with Stevie?" and immediately scolded himself for jumping to it too soon and risking giving away his plan.

"Huh? Oh, almost eight months... off and on. Okay, enough talk. We can talk later," Tim said before pulling a small silver flask from his suit jacket, screwing off the top, and taking a couple of gulps. Holding it up to Blue, the boy shook his head and then regretted it since he could've used it to calm down.

"Ya came prepared," Blue said.

"Yup, ya never knows when a shot'll come in handy."

"That's true," Blue said, appreciating the double entendre Tim unknowingly used. "Yeah, ya never knows when a shot'll come in handy. So... where?"

"Where what?"

"Where'd ya play with Stevie?"

"Oh... the car, the woods, my place when mom's out. Come on, enough talk. Let's get this party started."

"How many others, other kids?"

Tim smiled. "Are you jealous? Awww, that's cute. I'd like ta tell ya yer my first, but I'm thirty-one. There was a few before ya."

"Like Keith?"

"You knew about Keith too? Yeah, he and me played together."

"I guess 'e... they must've decided to quit, eh?"

"Come on, enough talk. Yer teasin' me. Ya can tease me next time," Tim said, again patting the sheet beside him. "Sit. We'll talk later. There'll be lots of time fer that."

Next time? There won't even be a first time!

Blue took a deep breath. "They decided to quit, eh? That's why ya killed 'em, so they wouldn't talk?"

Tim's eyes lost their excitement. "Huh? Who?"

"STEVIE AND KEITH!"

"What? No, nothin' like that! I didn't kills no one! Yer nervous... and scared. I gets that. The first date... the first time is always weird," he said, trying to tame his noticeable frustration. "Now, come on, let's play!"

Blue shouted, "I'M NOT GOIN' TO PLAY WITH YA, YA DAMN FREAK!"

With an intense look, Tim said, "Now don't tease me! You either give me what I wants or I'm goin' ta... I'm goin' ta take it!" Getting to his feet, he walked toward Blue. "Come here ya little shit... or... or I'll hook ya up with Stevie!" As Blue stepped back, a branch poked him in the back, and then towering over him, Tim grabbed his jacket and began unzipping it. "Ya really wanna test me, do ya?"

With the sound of a double metallic click confusing Tim, Blue pulled the cocked thirty-eight revolver from his pocket and pushed its muzzle against the man's chest.

"I came prepared too," Blue said in a desperately controlled voice. "Remember, ya never knows when a shot'll come in handy."

"Are ya kiddin' me?" Tim asked, releasing Blue's jacket and stepping back. "Now, relax with that thing. Its got a light trigger. Just stay cool."

"Sit down, ya perv! There... sit down there on the sheet!" demanded Blue, whose heart beat so hard that his entire body seemed to throb.

"Just keep yer cool. Keep cool," Tim pleaded as sweat accumulated on his forehead. "It's loaded? It's not loaded, eh?"

Blue pulled his other hand from his pocket and opened it to reveal two bullets in the palm of his hand. "Ya tell me! I said sit!"

Sitting on the bedsheet, Tim said, "Okay... okay, this is all fun and everythin', but let's puts that away and get outta here."

"So, yer the perv, the Kid Killer, right?" Blue asked, pointing the gun at his face.

"Hey, I didn't kills nobody," Tim said sheepishly. "Now stop pointin' that thing at me! If it goes off, it'll kill me!"

"Kill ya? What a shame that would be. Ya thinks there'd be anyone missin' ya... besides yer mommy? Everyone's goin' ta figure out yer the sick freak who's been doin' the killin's. If they don't, I'm goin' ta tell 'em. We'll see yer ass in Jail, and ya knows what they do ta pervs in jail."

"No! No, that's not me! No, not me! I just said that shit ta... ta scares ya!"

"Shut up! Not you? Ya perved Stevie, and now he's dead. They even found 'im almost naked!"

"Okay... okay... I played with Stevie but only played. I didn't kill 'im!"

"And Keith! What abouts Keith?"

Defeated, Tim put his hands down to his sides and whispered, "The same thing... I mean, I played with 'im, but I didn't kill 'im."

Blue stepped forward.

"So what's the story? You knew Keith and Stevie. So how'd ya finds the other one? Ya pick 'im off the street?"

"I didn't know 'im! I didn't kill 'im! I swears ta God!"

Blue stepped closer. "What does a perv like ya do when the guys refuses? Ya couldn't let 'em tell anyone, could ya? Nah, ya'd have ta shut 'em up for good!"

"No, I just threatened 'em, that's all... that's it!"

"Ya tellin' me that ya'd let 'em tell on ya. Is that what ya expects me ta believe? Ya'd let them get yer ass thrown in jail?"

"Shit, man! I didn't kill nobody! I didn't!"

"Stop looking at me, perv! Look away!" With Tim reluctantly turning his head away, Blue said, "I saw yer expression when ya knew it wasn't goin' ta happen. I could sees the anger in ya! Ya'd kill ta get whats ya wants!"

Turning to look at Blue, Tim's eyes went from pleading to glaring. "Look, ya little shit, I didn't kill nobody!" he said as he got to his knees and was about to stand.

"Sit the hell down! Sit down on yer ass!"

Continuing to glare at Blue, Tim paused before sitting back down.

Blue tried to focus his thoughts. So far he had improvised everything, but not the finish. He needed a finish. He needed to decide what to do. If he were to turn the freak in, how would he do it? At gunpoint? Should he run home, lock his door and call his dad first? Should he shoot Tim? Could he shoot him? He doubted he could pull the trigger on someone just sitting there, as Tim was. But if he shot him, would he try to make it look like a suicide, or would he say he was defending himself? Then noticing the revolver shaking in his hand, he instinctively closed his eyes and tried to calm down.

Seeing the opportunity, Tim jumped to his feet and tried to pull the gun from Blue's shaking hand.

Blue would never remember pulling the trigger — it was like the trigger pulled his finger — but he would remember the enormous blast.

Kneeling on the edge of the bedsheet, his ears rang, his trigger finger hurt and the flesh between it and his thumb hurt from the revolver's unexpected kick, which made him drop it on the sheet between him and Tim, who lay on his back with his feet tucked under him, one arm out to his side, the other back by his head where a circle of blood was slowly growing.

Blue struggled again to focus his thoughts, and after taking a moment to think, he picked up the gun, and while keeping the soles of his dress sneakers from touching the sheet, he crawled over to Tim, fumbled to put the gun in his hand, and then using his sleeve, wiped it clean of his fingerprints. Finished, he noticed his footprints on the edge of the sheet and patted them out. Standing up, he checked himself for blood, and not seeing any, he took a moment to think if there was anything he forgot. He had the sense to wipe the bullets clean of prints as he loaded them into the gun. He had gotten something out of those crime shows, but nothing about the power of the gun's kick and its deafening blast.

After a crack of thunder made him jump, he made his way toward Autumn Drive.

With his heart continuing to race, he tried to calm down, and it was only after forcing his mind back to the song *Bohemian Rhapsody* that he realized the irony of its lyrics.

CHAPTER 12
Greene's Dilemma

An answering machine with its light blinking, an electric typewriter, and four manila folders were the only things on his desk. On the floor to the left of it laid a stapler forced opened by the impact, a broken ceramic cup, several pens and pencils, a dozen blank forms revealing their triplicate pages separated by sheets of carbon paper, and his pistol, which he habitually placed on his desk whenever he entered his office and had never once fired in the line of duty and over the last few months, hadn't even fired in the soundproofed firing range within the basement of the station. Buried under it all was a smashed picture frame containing a not-so-recent photo of his now middle-aged wife and his three adolescent children, two boys and a girl who had since then graduated university. And sprinkled on top of the mess were dozens of miscellaneous papers, memos, and correspondences — one of which was the cause of the mess.

Chief Henderson had dropped in earlier that morning, placed an official-looking sheet of paper on Greene's desk, said, "You should read this," and left with a quick pat on Greene's shoulder.

The chief was stressed. Normally, he might have stayed for several minutes and chatted about nothing related to the job, and over those chats, the two had confided in each other about their struggles with alcohol, which seemed to come with the job, and both shared the belief that being in the company of other off-duty officers only pushed the temptation. Outside of work, neither socialized with other officers, so neither had any close friends.

Greene had read the letter and expected it was written by someone who had read Dale Carnegie's *How to Win Friends and Influence People*. It was a Help-Me-Help-You-To-Help-Me letter from the mayor's office, stating the city was under much pressure to close the Kid Killer case, the mayor understood the difficulties with the case, and their office was there to help in any way possible and was only waiting to be asked.

Greene was normally a cool-headed, objective detective who prided himself on his self-control, much like Detective Porfiry from *Crime and Punishment*, one of his favorite novels, but that morning something in him had snapped. Between the lines of the letter, he had read, *Solve this now, or you had better be prepared to explain your incompetence.* Without saying it in the letter, the mayor wanted the department to name Williams as the murderer, and Greene had lost it. After having cleared his desk of everything at the front of it, he had to force himself not to clear off the heavier items at the back before the anger vanished as suddenly as it had come.

In a few minutes, Greene had a meeting with the chief. They had to decide what to say about Timothy Williams. They had to decide if his death was a suicide and if he had been the Kid Killer. Both the chief and he wanted to agree on both counts, but there were dangling doubts.

The day before, Greene had checked Williams' car, hoping to find a blood-stained knife and a roll of duct tape, and found neither. But when he and several police officers had searched the home of Williams' mother, they discovered a bulging envelope taped to the back of his dresser, and in it was a collection of Polaroid photos of young boys in various poses, some partly dressed and others naked. Two of the boys were identified as Steven Kelly, the third victim, and Keith Murphy, the first. There were no photos of the second.

It was obvious Williams was a pedophile, but would that push him to murder? It wouldn't be the first time a pedophile murdered to cover his initial crime, but in all three cases, there was no sign of sexual assault, but there was a familiarity between the last victim and his killer that wasn't there with the others. Steven Kelly's death was drawn out. He was tortured before he was killed and there was an obvious sign that the killer had intended to continue the torture but had stopped prematurely and suffocated the child. The killer had played Tic-Tac-Toe in the flesh of the child's chest but had only got so far as to cut a bloody X in the center spot. Greene was sure that action, that type of torture, involved a level of passion that could only come from being familiar with the victim, much like one lover stabbing the other dozens of times.

With two of the three murder cases connected to Williams, Greene still couldn't shake off his hunch against closing them. He had learned to trust his hunches, and his hunch then was that there was still a killer out there.

Pulling from the top folder several sheets of paper held together by a staple, Greene sat back in the uncomfortable wooden chair and again read the Forensic report on Williams' death that stated it was a suicide but qualified it with a note that the weather had minimized the evidence.

Greene questioned the conclusion. If it was suicide, it was more likely an accidental suicide or a premature suicide. There was residual powder on both of Williams' hands, though more on his left than his right, making it seem that Williams, for some reason, had his left hand up by his head when he awkwardly pulled the trigger with his right. Awkwardly, because Williams was left-handed. It was unusual too to find a suicide weapon with fingerprints only where the person had held it to fire and none where the person had picked it up and handled it. Even its cylinder and rounds had been wiped clean. Then there was the entry wound; Williams had shot himself in the forehead while suicides by handgun are normally to the temple, up through the mouth, or under the chin. And to add to the awkwardness of the suicide, because of the lack of burned flesh at the bullet's entry point, Williams would've held the gun away from his head when most suicidal shots to the head involve holding the gun directly to it, though Forensics couldn't conclude exactly how far. And what was with the bedsheet? If he planned to kill himself, why use a sheet? Sure, it's common for a person to remove a watch and perhaps eyeglasses, and some even cleaned their residence beforehand, but to bring a bedsheet into the forest, that was going to the extreme. Was he concerned about dirtying his suit pants for his upcoming funeral?

Even though there were no telltale signs of murder (restraint marks, bruising, and other signs of a struggle), from a planned suicide perspective, it made little sense to Greene. If there had been a suicide note, he could've ignored all the discrepancies for a small fee of doubt.

Greene placed the Forensic report back in the folder and dropped it on his desk. Leaving his chair, he kneeled next to the mess, picked up his handgun, slid it into his shoulder holster, and began gathering the forms, trying to make a neat pile out of them. Stopping, he dropped them to the floor. He had more reason than not to leave the mess. He could use it as a reminder of his abnormal outburst and he could use it as a warning to other staff not to disturb him frivolously, like the detectives in Narcotics, who would enter his office to brag about their weekend sexual exploits.

Greene thought it strange how he had forgotten how stressful Homicide could be. It had been several years since he had felt the heavy pressure, and he craved a drink.

Grabbing the folders, he took a deep breath and left the office.

As a barrage of flashes welcomed them into the room, Greene and one police officer followed behind their boss, who, with what looked like a victory smile, walked up to the podium while Greene and the officer stood several feet behind him.

Without looking directly at anyone, the chief cleared his throat and said, "Welcome, folks. I'll make this short. We have a strong reason to believe Timothy Williams of Spryfield was the Kid Killer, as you had earlier labeled it. We found Williams in possession of homemade child pornography, which included two of the three victims, and since Williams had committed suicide soon after the murder of the last child, we can only speculate he did it because he knew we were on to him."

Before he could ask for questions, the impatient press volleyed a burst of them.

"You there, Mike."

"Thank you. Sir, what would you say is the probability of Williams being the Kid Killer?"

"Well... I think it would be safe to say it's close to... to ninety-five percent." He looked back at Greene. "Would you say that's about correct, Detective Greene?" Forced on the spot, Greene stiffly nodded his head, and before the small crowd could volley its next burst of questions, the chief asked, "Chris from the *Mail Star*, is it? Yes?"

"What are you doing to bring that probability to one hundred percent?"

"Good question. We'll be cleaning up any loose ends we have regarding suspects and we'll be delving deeper into Williams' past, which may lead us to more evidence. We know Williams spent some time in Toronto and only arrived back in Halifax months before the murders began, so we'll be working with the Toronto Police Department to see if they can connect him to any missing children there or any open cases involving their murders. Okay... one last question and then we'll be leaving."

As more questions flew at him, he said, "John, what's your question?"

"Sir, last time you held a press conference, you stated there was no serial killer and now you're saying there is... or was. What changed your mind?"

"Well... uh, we stated last time that the murders were inconsistent, which went against your standard serial killer's pattern. We now believe the inconsistencies resulted from spontaneous killings. Williams was a pedophile, of that we're certain, and we don't believe he intended to kill his victims, and when he did, he used whatever was close to him. As I had stated previously, serial killers plan their kill, while Williams, we expect, planned his sexual assaults but improvised the killings, going against the profile of... of what, I suppose, we would call a standard serial killer, but a serial killer regardless. Okay... that's all for now. Thank you for coming."

With more questions flying at them, Chief Henderson, Greene, and the officer walked out.

Greene was disappointed with the route taken by his boss, but he was grateful that he still had the five percent to work with, thanks to the press, and he would work with it. With the third victim, he had three suspects: Williams, François Roy, and Avriel Rosen, but with Williams dead, he had only two, and if nothing came out of those and the killings ceased, he would have to accept Williams was the Kid Killer.

Both Roy and Rosen were connected to the first and last victims. Roy knew the first and last, and Rosen knew the third but only had a connection with the first through its discovery. But then some killers craved the limelight, and some of those had even written letters to their local papers, pointing out the location of their latest victim. Maybe Rosen had changed his mind about concealing the first body. Maybe he craved the limelight and needed the first body found. Greene thought it possible that Roy could've worked with Williams, but Rosen would be working alone. It was difficult to imagine the old man working with anyone.

Then Greene thought about how things would've been different if the killer had chosen to kill outside the poorer neighborhoods. The parents in those lower-class neighborhoods gave their children much more freedom, making them more vulnerable to abduction, and the murders were bound to, at least initially, receive less attention from the media. If the killings had occurred in the middle or upper-class areas, all hell would've broken loose after the discovery of the first victim and the media would've begun following the case more closely. The city would've felt more pressure earlier to deal with the situation, would've placed more police patrols in the area, and most likely would've organized a group of officers to go door to door distributing flyers warning of a murderer in the area, all so the department would be seen as proactive. Greene expected too that the residents in those areas would've done something like a children's watch group.

Back in his office, Greene found on his desk two triplicate request forms returned with a judge's signature on each and their middle sheets gone. Content, he pulled out their two sheets of carbon paper and picked up his phone's receiver to arrange for a group of patrol officers to accompany him.

CHAPTER 13
A Loose End

It was early Thursday morning, three days after the discovery of Tim's body, when a heavy pounding finally caught Avriel's attention. Initially, he thought it was thunder accompanying the rush of heavy rain against the bathroom window, and it was only because of its rhythm (three quick pounds repeated several times) that he realized someone was at his front door... and they were desperate to speak to him.

Hurrying down the stairs while tightening his bathrobe, Avriel unlocked and opened the door to find Detective Greene in a wet overcoat standing in front of four uniformed police officers who were just as wet. Over the shoulders of two of the officers, he saw a police car silently pull up in front of his house and park behind two other police cars.

"Mr. Rosen, we have a warrant to search your premises."

Avriel's jaw dropped. For a moment, he thought he was dreaming or, more appropriately, having a nightmare.

"Sir, we don't need your permission to enter."

"Right... right," Avriel said, trying to collect himself before he moved to the side and the five men entered, followed seconds later by two more. The last one to enter forced two others to move out of his way as he closed the door.

Greene unfolded and held out a sheet of paper. "We need

you to stay here and out of our way until we're finished."

"What... what are you searching for?" Avriel asked, taking the paper and glancing at it before Greene snatched it back.

"You tell us!" demanded an officer whom Avriel didn't recognize, though he recognized two uncomfortable faces from the year before and may have greeted them if not for the situation.

"I... I wish I knew," was all Avriel could get out.

"Guys, start in the living room. Mr. Rosen, come with me. I have some questions for you."

With the officers heading into the living room, their shoes squeaking as their wet rubber soles made contact with the hardwood floor, the detective led Avriel into what he assumed correctly was the kitchen, where the two sat across from each other at the small hardwood table.

"Mr. Rosen, I need your car keys, and you could save us some time by telling us where you have some quarter-inch rope and a roll of duct tape."

"No... no rope, but... but I have gray duct tape in the... in the bottom drawer there," Avriel said, pointing his shaking finger toward the four drawers below the counter.

The detective stood up, went to the counter, pulled out the deeper bottom drawer, and rummaged through it before retrieving an almost full roll of duct tape that had its end evenly cut with scissors.

"I... I last used it to seal a broken window last summer," Avriel said as the detective examined the roll and placed it back in the drawer. "And I'll have to go upstairs for the car keys."

"And I'll have to go with you," Greene informed him.

In his bedroom, Avriel retrieved his keys from the bureau, handed them to the detective, and spotted Sam's tail sticking out from under the bed.

After checking the bathroom, including the inside of the toilet's tank, Greene allowed Avriel to change into a pair of pants and a shirt, and as he did, Greene called down to an officer, tossed down Avriel's keys, and told him he had checked the upstairs bathroom.

Minutes later, Avriel and Greene returned to their kitchen chairs where Greene took out a pen and a small notepad from his suit jacket, turned to a fresh page, and stared intensely into Avriel's eyes, hoping for a sign of panic but seeing only confusion. "So... Mr. Rosen, what's your relationship with the Dixons... Lisa and Dwight Dixon?"

"They are my friends... my close friends."

"Just friends? Nothing more intimate with Lisa Dixon? Isn't she single... or a widow now?"

The question startled Avriel. "Yes... I mean, yes, she is a widow, and no, nothing sexual, if that is what you are asking."

Content that he had got a reaction out of the old man, Greene asked, "Isn't she a widow because of you?"

Startled by that question too, Avriel said, "It... it depends on how you look at it, I suppose."

"Her husband died in this house, no? He fell down your stairs, no? Crushed his neck against the wall beside the door back there?"

"Yes, yes, he did. My cat interfered with his attempt to hurt... kill me. You had seen the ripped stocking on his head, the many cat scratches on his face."

"Right, I did, but why did he attack you? He had no convictions and no previous conflict with you besides that incident outside *his* home... that same night, your wife passed away. Maybe an affair with his wife?"

"No. I had told you then that I believe he did not like us... like Jews befriending his wife and child. My wife had befriended them, and he went mad when he found out. That was the same night when... when Lisa kicked him out. A few days later, he painted the words, *One down, one to go,* on my front door and sent a rock through my window with the same message. Why... why are you only questioning me now after just yesterday saying you had caught the killer? I am assuming this has to do with the killings... unless you reopened the case on Paul Dixon's death."

Greene hid his frustration with the returned questions by writing in his notebook and then laughing. A laugh he had practiced. A laugh he hoped would get a rise out of Rosen, making him angry enough to speak without thinking.

"I do not see what is humorous. Why are you asking me these questions and going through my home?"

"We're not re-examining Mr. Dixon's death, and yes, we believe we caught... or have discovered who the killer was. And you should've heard we're ninety-five percent sure, which means you're part of the five percent. I'm only one man, so forgive me for only getting to you now. This is also the third time we are meeting, no? The third time I'm questioning you regarding a death, or in this case, three. That certainly raises alarms, no?"

"Right," Avriel said in a defeated tone.

"Tell me, how does an old man become close friends with a young mother of a nine-year-old boy?"

Avriel didn't appreciate being called an old man by a man maybe ten years younger, and then it occurred to him that Greene was trying to upset him, and he tried answering calmly, "Dewey is ten now. They were my wife's friends, and I became closer to them after her death."

"And because you were friends, Mr. Dixon painted the message on your door and then tried to kill you? It seems such a minor reason to kill someone."

"I suppose, but you would have to ask him."

"Right. I would, but obviously can't. Okay... so, Avriel... can I call you Avriel?"

"No."

"Okay, why did you move into this neighborhood? You used to live on Jubilee Road, no? Any financial problems?"

"Yes, we moved here two winters back. My wife felt we needed to move to a smaller place. And no, we have no financial problems."

"I see. Aren't there smaller places on Jubilee? Why here?"

"She liked the neighborhood."

As Greene turned a page and began writing again, Avriel glanced down to see if he could read any of the writing from upside down, but it was illegible.

Greene looked up from his notes and noticed the change in the old man. His face had gone expressionless and his eyes became cold. Shifting in his chair, Greene looked around for anything the old man could easily grab and use as a weapon. There was nothing obvious, so the detective took advantage of the moment by pushing the old man further. "You like this neighborhood, right? All those children running by your place. I suppose no kids ran in front of your window on Jubilee."

"Look here, if you are going to hint, you may say it directly."

"Really? Is that right? Okay, let me put it another way. You certainly have an interest in Dwight and it appears you had an interest in Steven. Mrs. Kelly tells me you took the kids to the movies every weekend. Dwight, Steven, and Bartholomew, or Blue, I guess it is. A strange name, no?"

Greene noticed the old man was perspiring heavily and breathing fast, and he enjoyed it. The more he pushed and the more Rosen reacted to it, the more chance of a confession.

"No. I heard of Violet, Amber, and Little Boy Blue," Avriel said, repeating Dewey's words from the day they met

Blue. "Perhaps you should arrest me and allow me to contact my lawyer."

"Fine, maybe that's what we'll have to do," Greene replied in a condescending tone. "I still have a few more questions for you. Should I arrest you or will you answer them here? The guys will be done soon and your day can go on as usual."

Having stopped paying attention to their noises, Avriel had almost forgotten about the other officers. Then, listening, he heard them in the living room, in the basement, and upstairs, and when he looked toward the dining room, he saw its table flipped on its side and an officer checking the bottom.

"Then finish and be done with it," Avriel said, surprised by his own aggressive posturing.

Greene was content with Rosen's decision. He had no interest in arresting him, or more importantly, no solid evidence for an arrest, although he hoped that would change in the next few minutes.

"Let's see... let's see... right," Greene said as he checked over his notes and then flipped to the next blank page. "Let's talk about the day you discovered the body of Keith Murphy. What were you doing there in the woods, those woods?"

"As I told you then, I was playing catch with Lisa and Dewey and I had batted the ball in among the trees."

"You play there often?"

"No, it was the first time... and the last."

"Great, thank you. And you went to that particular ball diamond because?"

"Because it was the closest."

"No, it wasn't. It isn't the closest."

Avriel wiped his head.

"Why are you sweating, Mr. Rosen?"

"Because I am nervous. I would think that would be obvious."

"Why are you nervous? I'm just asking you simple questions?"

"It's not every day that I am interrogated," Avriel said, trying to control his frustration. "Where is the closest?"

"Closest what?"

"Closest diamond. You had just said the one we went to was not the closest."

"Did I?" Greene pretended to forget. "Oh, right I did. Yes, there is a much closer one just at the top of Cowie Hill up there," he said, gesturing with his head toward Herring Cove Road.

When Avriel swallowed, Greene hoped he was going to break down and say something incriminating, but, instead, he asked, "May I... May I get up to get a glass of water?"

Staring intensely at his suspect, Greene's ears were reddening as they always did when he became impatient. "When we're done. We're almost done."

Empty-handed, the officers began appearing at the kitchen's entrance.

Greene cleared his throat. "Well, would you look at that? They've finished already. Let's let them search the kitchen. With that many, they'll be done in a sec."

After a drenched officer handed Avriel's car keys to Greene and shook his head, Green directed Avriel to get up. Then after the two moved to the dining room table, the officers swarmed the kitchen, pulling out drawers and searching the cupboards.

Laying Rosen's keys on the table, Greene raised his voice over the noise in the kitchen, "Guys, I'll meet you at the door when you're done, and the duct tape in the larger drawer is the wrong color," and turning again to Avriel, he asked, "So tell me again how you found Keith Murphy?"

"I told you this before, back when it had happened. I had

been looking for the baseball. I had hit it too hard, and it went into the forest."

Greene wrote into his pad and then looked up, puzzled. "The body was covered with rocks, right?"

Avriel nodded.

"How did you find it?"

"The smell. I recognized it and searched for the source."

"The smell? You recognized it? How's that?"

"It... it was the smell of a rotting corpse. It was common throughout the war. A person does not forget that smell."

"Right... the war." Greene laid the pen down and looked at the old man curiously. "What exactly does a rotting corpse smell like? I can't imagine it smelled like roses."

"You... you do not know? You did not smell it when I pointed the body out to you and the others? I remember you holding your hand over your nose. If you had to hold your nose, you must have smelled it."

Ignoring Avriel's response, Greene shifted in his seat. "So, Mr. Rosen, the sixty-four thousand dollar question, where were you on May fifteenth, the week after Mother's Day?"

"Home, I was here with Dewey. We played a television game and ordered pizza. You can confirm it with the delivery chap."

"Okay, but what about after that? I know you dropped off Dwight at around seven and I know Steven left Bartholomew's apartment around that time. So where did you go after that? What did you do?"

"I went home and stayed there."

"Any witnesses? Anyone to validate that?"

"Sam."

"Who's Sam?"

"My cat."

"Right, the cat. That's cute. I talked to your neighbors.

Some are certain you've got something to do with the killings and none remember seeing your car parked that evening. That doesn't mean it wasn't there, but I do find it interesting how you almost ran Dwight down with your car last summer, fought with his father a couple of months later, and a few months after that, found the first murdered child, and then... and then another few months later, Paul Dixon dies in your home, this house."

"That is all true. There have been some strange happenings, except for running down Dewey. He rode his bike into the side of my car. I was turning right... there was a sun shower. He slid directly into the side of my car."

"Right," Greene said, and then, feeling like he was getting nowhere and would get nowhere, he stood up and put his notepad and pencil back in his pocket. "Oh, one more thing. Why did you pay for Steven Kelly's funeral?"

"Excuse me?" Avriel asked, surprised by the question.

"You paid for his funeral. Mr. Parker at Parker's funeral home told me so. Why did you do that?"

"I do not know exactly."

"Well now, Mr. Rosen, you were doing so fine with the questions, and now you tell me you don't know why you did something. You don't know why you paid almost thirty-seven hundred dollars. Really? Maybe it was guilt?"

"Maybe."

"Maybe?"

"Maybe it was the guilt of being a Have around Have Nots," Avriel admitted.

Frustrated, Greene stood up. "Okay, that's it. Don't be upset with Mr. Parker. He told me you wanted to keep your generosity a secret, but I'm the police, after all. Now I have to buy these boys breakfast, seeing how I got them up bright and early this morning, and in the rain at that," Greene chuckled.

"Heck, I got you up bright and early too. You want to come with us?" With Avriel saying nothing, he said, "We'll show ourselves out. No reason to get up. Hey, I noticed the sale sign in front of your house. You're moving? Maybe out of the city, the province, the country? Planning on running away, are you?"

Again, Avriel said nothing.

"Oh, one more tiny thing. I need you to humor me. Did you kill the children?"

Avriel's eyes widened and his voice rose, "No!"

"Did you kill one of them, at least?"

"No!"

"I need you to say it. Spell it out for me if you would."

Avriel took a deep breath and said in almost a whisper, "I did not kill the children. I did not kill *any* of the children. I am not... not a murderer."

Greene forced a fake smile. "Right, right, well, thanks for that. You have a good day now," he said, and after he left to join the group of officers waiting at the door, Avriel looked past the entrance and into the living room, where he could see a mess of books on the floor and several bookcases pulled out from the walls. Realizing his hands hurt, he looked down and noticed for the first time that his hands were clutching the edge of the table. When he released his grip, his hands automatically made a loose fist, and then, forcibly and painfully, he stretched out the reluctant digits.

After Greene and the officers left the house and he heard the vehicles drive away, a mentally exhausted Avriel forced himself to get up and go to the front door to lock it before making his way up the stairs to pacify Sam.

By the time eleven-thirty came around, Avriel had showered and changed, tidied up the house, and was ready to pick up Dewey for lunch, and as he opened the door, a huge wave of anxiety hit him. He didn't want to be outside, and he didn't want to be around people.

Then he noticed his wife's perfume.

CHAPTER 14
Another Loose End

Tired, Frank fiddled with his key to open the inside glass door and enter the apartment building.

For the last two weeks, he hadn't been his usual self. He was quiet, reflective, and melancholic. His son's best friend, a child Frank had known for years, had been murdered, making it two children he was familiar with who were murdered in the last six months, and then soon after, Tim had killed himself with Frank's gun. He assumed it was his, since after the suicide, he discovered the smaller gun was missing. Then soon after that, they declared Tim the killer of the children. And to add to his state, the previous day Lisa had come to his door to hug him, thankful that their sons had escaped death. She was certain it would've been one of the two next, or maybe, since they spent so much time together, both. She didn't say it, but he expected she was blaming him for trusting Tim around the boys.

That weekend past, before Tim's body was discovered, he felt something was wrong when his friend's car was parked in his spot over the weekend, and when he called Tim's mother that Sunday night, she hadn't seen or heard from him either, but she wasn't worried since he had a habit of disappearing for days.

He still had difficulty accepting that Tim had committed suicide and was both a pedophile and a killer, but that difficulty was mostly because of his reluctance to admit that the man he thought he knew almost as well as himself, he didn't know at all, making him feel he was guilty by association and making it difficult to be out in public and even to make eye contact with anyone besides his son.

It was only at work the night before that it occurred to him he had been ignoring Blue's feelings. He was a tough kid, but he was still a kid and Stevie's death followed by the death of Tim, and then the news of Tim killing Stevie must have added to the boy's stress just as it was adding to his.

Frank entered his apartment, tossed his workbag on the sofa, and met Blue at the small table near the kitchen.

"Bon matin," Blue greeted him as he was about to eat his bowl of cornflakes.

"Bon matin, Mon Cheri."

"Comment ça va?"

Frank placed his arm around his son's neck. "Oh, you know... same old, same old," he replied before sniffing the air. "Hey, you smell something funny?"

Blue inhaled through his nose and cringed. "Yeah! Ya just farted, and it ain't funny! I'm eatin' here!"

Frank released Blue and sniffed again. "Nope, wasn't me, had to be you. You smell it, you own it. Hey, I was thinking we might do something this weekend. Maybe we can go on a short trip. I was thinking we drive over to New Brunswick and visit Magnetic Hill. We could stay over and come back on Sunday. Maybe we could even visit Grandpa if we think we can put up with him for an hour or so."

Blue's eyes lit up. "That sounds cool! Can we bring Dwight?"

"I was thinking we do a father and son thing. Besides, I

don't think Lisa would allow it. I'm on her bad side... for now, anyway."

"I hear ya. We haven't gone anywhere in a while. That sounds like—"

A sudden pounding on the door froze both for a second. Normally they would've yelled for Tim to come in since he often pulled the stunt of knocking aggressively on the door and then entering and asking which one pissed their pants, but Tim was dead. The residual effect of his death was the repeat visits from the police and then the detective, but even then, after ringing the buzzer, they knocked politely.

With a second pounding at the door, Frank shouted, "Un moment!" and just as he turned and sprinted past the kitchen toward his bedroom, the door opened and Detective Greene stepped in.

"Christ!" Blue exclaimed.

"Don't move!" ordered Greene with his revolver pointed at Frank, who stood near the entrance to his bedroom.

As a group of uniformed officers with their weapons out assembled behind him, Greene shoved his revolver into his shoulder holster, and from inside of his suit jacket, he pulled out a folded sheet of paper and held it up. "François Roy, I have a warrant to search your apartment. Put your hands up and walk toward us," he said, gesturing with the paper.

Frank did as he was told, and when he reached the officers, they patted him down and ordered him to wait there, and after another officer searched between the cushions of the sofa, he gestured for Frank to sit there.

For the first time in a long time, Frank had to force himself to speak English. "What's... what's this all about?" he asked with a more prominent accent than usual.

Expecting to be searched too, Blue dropped the spoon into the bowl and nervously stood up.

"Cleaning up loose ends related to Timothy Williams. You knew him, no?"

"You know I did," Frank said meekly, making Blue realize something was very wrong. "Blue, go to Lisa's until these men leave. He can wait at Lisa's... Mrs. Dixon's, right?"

"Sure. She's down the hall, right? I don't see why not, but we'll have to check him."

Not saying a word, Blue walked to the door and stood there as a police officer quickly patted him down, and as he left, he gave his dad a fearful glance back.

Detective Greene couldn't have been any more content with their surprise appearance. The morning's surprise searches were the best. Any emergency plan a suspect may have had for such an event most likely couldn't be acted on, and as surprise searches go, this was perfect. Greene knew François was driving Tim's car — he was trying to sell it for Tim's mother — and Greene knew when Frank would leave work for home. All they needed to do was watch him leave and then, two minutes later, head to his home. Making sure Tim's car was sitting in his parking space, the small parade of police cars had parked on the side of the street just far enough from the building so as not to be seen from the apartment's ground-level windows.

"Okay, two to a bedroom and two to the living room," Greene said to the officers before sitting down beside Frank while two officers searched in front of them.

Before Greene had a chance to talk, Frank said, "I'm not saying anything without my lawyer."

"Well, then I guess we'll just quietly sit here until the search is done. I need your car keys, Williams' and yours. Is this bag yours?"

Frank nodded, pulled out two sets of keys from his pocket, and offered them to Greene, who looked through the bag before handing the keys to an officer. "My black Trans Am is in the visitor parking round back," Frank said as the officer left the apartment.

They had sat for almost ten minutes, both listening to the noises in the other rooms while watching the search of the few pieces of furniture and electronics in front of them, when from Frank's bedroom, an officer yelled out to Greene, whose eyes lit up. Jumping to his feet and giving Frank a facetious thumbs-up and a wink of an eye, he left, yelling for an officer to watch the man.

In the bedroom, Greene was glad to find two officers proudly displaying their findings. One held two tightly compressed plastic-wrapped bundles, each the size of a clay brick, and a half-full black garbage bag of loose material. The other held the Colt revolver box with the Luger and two boxes of bullets resting on top.

"Weed," said the officer holding the bundles.

"A luger, an empty revolver box, and two packs of ammo, different sizes," said the other.

Detective Greene had little interest in the weed, but the empty pistol box interested him, and he hoped the serial number on the box would match the gun Williams used, though it would most likely not change much of anything.

"Cuff him!" Greene yelled toward the living room and then said to the officers in front of him, "Good work. Keep looking. If there's that much weed, there's certain to be cash around."

Joining Frank, who was then sitting on the sofa with his hands behind him, Green nodded to the officer to leave before sitting beside the French Canadian.

"You know what we found?"

Frank said nothing.

"Lots of marijuana. The officers are looking for your stash

of cash now. Every drug dealer has a stash, right? Do you have a restricted weapons license?"

Frank shook his head.

"Right, so we also have you on illegal firearms possession."

Frank finally spoke. "Is that what you're searching for? Is that what's on the warrant? If not, then you can't charge me."

Greene smiled. "You watch too much American TV. You should probably know that in Canada if we find evidence of a different major crime other than what we're looking for, we still charge. Our laws don't favor the criminals as much as they do in the US. Too bad for you, no? And before you mention it, we also don't have a second amendment."

With Frank dropping his eyes to the floor defeated, two officers who had searched Blue's room entered the living room and shook their heads.

"Okay, take the... the *gentleman* to the car. We'll sort out the charges at the station."

As two police officers lifted the stone-faced Frank to his feet by his restrained arms and walked him to the door, the two officers who were searching Frank's room appeared, holding their earlier finds with the addition of two bundles of bills.

"Great!" Greene said. "Take the stuff to the car and mark them. I'll meet you guys at the station."

Greene was the last to leave the apartment. Closing the door, he was about to head up the flight of stairs when a woman's voice called out to him, causing him to turn around and find Lisa coming toward him.

"What's going on? Where's Frank going? Blue told me you barged into his apartment."

"That's right, Mrs. Dixon. He's been arrested. Now, with all the excitement, I forgot all about the boy. We'll have Children's Services come by your place today. Mr. Roy will see a judge on Monday morning but don't expect to see him out on bail. It's his third time and by far the most serious, so the crown will probably argue against it, seeing how he's from New Brunswick, and that most likely makes him a flight risk. Goodbye and have a good day."

As Greene turned and walked up the stairs, Lisa stood there for a moment, stunned.

In her apartment, she found Dewey and Blue sitting quietly on the sofa, and taking Blue into her bedroom, she asked him what he had seen that morning and how he expected Frank might have broken the law.

Blue reluctantly informed her about his father selling marijuana, but he never thought about mentioning the guns. He never considered they were illegal.

Lisa had failed to notice any hint of Frank selling drugs, and she successfully held back the shock upon hearing it and her questions regarding it. Instead, she forced her attention on Blue, and feeling his family would be his best support and knowing his mother had disappeared, she asked him about his grandparents and learned that those on his mother's side lived in LaSalle, a predominantly Irish town on the island of Montreal, whom the young redhead had met once or twice. He never met Frank's mother, who had passed away before he was born, but Frank's father still lived in Fredericton, New Brunswick. Blue described him as a crazy old countryman who lived in a two-room shack in the forest where he hunted and fished. The boy's two uncles, Frank's brothers, lived in the States. He thought it was New York, but it could've been New Jersey or both.

**

At school that day, Blue was anxious. Several times, without being fully conscious of it, he began tapping his fingers on the desk, softly at first and then progressively harder until his teacher had to ask him to stop. Blue's behavior worried his teacher since nothing normally upset the easygoing youth, and at lunch that afternoon, Blue was the subject of discussion in the teachers' room. His teachers appreciated a break from his classroom shenanigans, but if Blue's emotional state was to worsen, they elected Mr. Ferguson, a fourth-grade teacher and the only male teacher Blue had experience with, to talk to him.

The rumors about his father wouldn't reach them until the next week.

**

Dewey spent the morning unable to focus on his schooling. After Stevie's death, he returned to school eager to learn and get his mind off the death of his friend, but that day his mind was on Blue's predicament. It seemed by his mother's questions, which he had eavesdropped on, that Frank wouldn't be coming home soon. It was one thing to have your father leave your home and have him visit weekly, as his father did for a short time before his death, but to have him leave and not see him for years would be awful. And to make things even worse, it was bad enough to lose one parent, but to lose both would make Blue an orphan, at least until his father returned, and Dewey knew from the novel *Oliver Twist*, which he and Avriel had slowly read together, that orphans were sent to an orphanage, or what in the book they called a workhouse, a not-so-nice place.

Besides being worried about Blue, Dewey was worried about himself. He had already lost one of his three best buddies and now he might lose another. If that happened, he wouldn't want any more of them. He could do without making them, only to lose them soon after.

CHAPTER 15
One Visitor, One Guest

At around eleven thirty, Lisa received a knock on her door, and as she opened it, she wanted to kick herself for forgetting to look through the peephole. Expecting to find Mrs. Publicover wanting to know what had happened to Frank, there was instead a woman in her early forties wearing a gray dress suit and looking slightly nervous.

"Hello. Mrs. Dixon?"

"Yes."

"Hi. I'm... I'm Mrs. Blakey from Children's Services. I'm here to pick up Bartholomew Roy."

"Oh... hi. Okay... well, come in, please," Lisa said as she moved aside to allow the woman to enter. "It's Blue. He likes to be called Blue. He... he won't be here for another half hour. He thought it best to go to school this morning to get his mind off the situation." With both standing by the closed door, Lisa added, "You can wait here if you'd like. Could I make you a coffee? Would you like a coffee?"

"Sure, that would be fine. Thank you."

Lisa directed Mrs. Blakey to the table and after finding out how her visitor took her coffee, made two. Then as the women sat across from each other, both equally uncomfortable, Mrs. Blakey looked at her watch before wrapping both hands around her mug, lifting it to her mouth, and taking a sip. "That's good coffee. Half an hour, you say? After I finish this, I should probably go wait in the car. I have to catch up on my paperwork. It's pretty bad when I think of my car as an office on wheels."

"Do you spend a lot of time on the road?"

The woman nodded. "It's a lot of interviewing... and then there's the picking up and dropping off of the children."

"It must be more than a bit stressful."

She nodded again. "But it's one of those jobs where you know you're doing some good."

"Right," Lisa nodded.

For the next minute, the two women drank their coffee in silence, both looking down at their mugs between sips. Then Lisa broke the silence by asking, "Uh... where will you be taking Blue?"

"We have a place downtown for children in his situation, where they wait for placement in the FPP, the Foster Parents Program."

It was the second time that day that Lisa had heard the word *foster*. Earlier that morning, Blue had commented that his punishment for everything was to be placed in a foster home. Lisa didn't know what a foster home was, and she didn't ask. She could only tell Blue that he wouldn't be punished for the crimes of his father. Hearing the word again concerned her, if only because it concerned Blue.

"What do you do with them while they wait?"

"We house them together. They sleep together. They get chores given to them, and of course, they have their playtime. Children in Bartho... Blue's situation aren't your... well, not your normal children, *per se*. Most have some sort of anti-social behavioral problems, but their stay with us isn't long, not usually more than a couple of months. I've seen toddlers go to homes after only three days. It's a great program, but sadly, it's always growing. We try to choose couples who have a natural nurturing ability."

"It sounds nice, but if I wanted Blue to stay with us, how'd I go about doing that?"

Mrs. Blakey looked down at her mug for a second. "Well, uh... you could apply to the program and then after a bit, if you're accepted, we'd see about transferring him here. But the problem would be your situation."

"What's my situation?" Lisa asked, trying to hide her offense with the assumption.

"Well, it's almost impossible to be a foster parent if you're on welfare."

"I'm not on welfare. I work full-time. I'm a cashier at Marvin's Groceries up the street."

Mrs. Blakey's face reddened slightly. "Oh, I'm sorry. I assumed a single mother... well, good for you."

"Uh... thank you. So you said after a bit. What's a bit?"

"Two months, maybe longer," Mrs. Blakey said, and then glanced at her watch. "Summer's on its way and that slows things down with vacations and all."

"Well, there must be another way, a faster way. I can tell you now Blue doesn't have any sort of behavioral problems. That's what you called it, right?"

"Anti-social behavioral problems, yes."

"He definitely doesn't have any of those."

"I'm sure he doesn't," Mrs. Blakey said in a patronizing tone. "There is another way, but it's rather more committed. If you were to have François Roy sign a legal document giving you temporary guardianship of Blue while he's incarcerated, it would give you the power to keep him in your care and increase your welfare check to pay for his needs."

"Remember, I work," Lisa reminded her guest.

The woman cracked an awkward smile. "Right. You'll have to excuse me. It's an assumption that's difficult to drop. Well, let's do that then," she said, bringing her mug up to her lips, taking a sip, and placing it back on the table. Standing up, she pushed her chair in. "I guess I should get my paperwork caught up. I'll be back in, let's say, fifteen minutes to take Blue with me, just until you have the papers signed."

Lisa stood up. "Could you let him stay here until I get it signed next week? I mean, why cause the boy more stress by taking him away to a strange place only to bring him back again?"

"Right. Uh... Mrs. Dixon, may I ask you how many children you have?"

"One."

"Listen, I can see you mean well, I really can, but I'm afraid you may find twice as many children too much and call me over the weekend to pick him up. If anything, I can take him today so he's calmed down when we bring him back... if you have the signed papers. I can certainly imagine just how stressed the child must be right now."

Fearing Blue was going to be taken to the last place he wanted to go, Lisa panicked. "No. No, I can help him better. I mean, he trusts me. He's great with my son and is very respectful. Your image of him is wrong, just wrong. He's a good boy... and smart. A great boy who could be something."

Lisa's concern moved the woman and for a moment, she washed away her habit of negative stereotyping and forced herself to see the woman in front of her not as a welfare case, which was so common in the area, but as a woman, a mother, her peer who was truly concerned about the boy's welfare.

"I'm concerned about his welfare just as much if not more than you... your department," Lisa pleaded. "I know Blue well. Maybe we can help each other to... to help him? If you were a mother, you'd understand."

"I *am* a mother. So I guess we're even now," Mrs. Blakey said, breaking a genuine smile as she straightened her jacket. "Mrs. Dixon, I'll tell you what. I'll leave him with you for a week and if you get the papers signed and still feel comfortable with your decision, we'll go from there. We'll treat it as if Blue's your guest. Let's make an appointment to get together a week from now, next Friday at eleven."

"Oh, thank you, thank you so much, Mrs. Blakey!" Lisa said and then impulsively hugged her visitor tightly. With the Children's Services woman's body stiffening up, Lisa released her and awkwardly took a step back.

"Well, uh, well... Mrs. Dixon, it's not the normal way we do things, but you strike me as a woman of good character. I should go but will see you a week from today. Oh... I should get your phone number," she said before reaching into her suit pocket, pulling out a small notebook, and writing in it as Lisa gave her the number. "And here's my card. Now call me if you have any problems."

At the door, Lisa thanked Mrs. Blakey again, but without a hug.

Earlier that morning, Lisa had called to inform Avriel of the incident. Hearing about the arrest, her older friend was taken aback, and he hid his disgust when learning Frank sold drugs, but he was glad he wasn't the only one searched, though it did place him, he felt unjustly, in the same group as a drug dealer.

During lunch at Lisa's, while the four silently ate MacDonald's cheeseburgers and fries, Avriel tried to make light of the situation. "Blue, I wish your father would have come to me for advice. I could have shown him how to do it without getting in trouble. You know, I sold drugs at seven different spots for almost thirty years and not one arrest, not one." With Lisa laughing while both boys just stared at him, he said, "I was a pharmacist. I owned drugstores. What do they teach you in school? After lunch, I'm speaking to your teachers."

After they finished eating but still sitting at the table, Lisa informed them of Mrs. Blakey's visit, and for the short term, Blue and Dewey would share Lisa's bed while she slept in Dewey's smaller one.

At a loss for words, Blue sat glossy-eyed, causing an excited Dewey to joke that Blue needed a tissue, and where Blue would've joked back with something like, "When I'm done with you, you'll need a few," he didn't, and his silence embarrassed Dewey.

Lisa's decision didn't surprise Avriel, who would've been surprised if she had let the boy go with Children's Services, and he volunteered to have his lawyer draw up the guardianship papers and have them signed by Frank.

That evening, after supper and to make Blue comfortable in his new surroundings, Lisa suggested he call her Lisa instead of Mrs. Dixon, and Avriel followed her gesture by suggesting he call him Av instead of Mr. Rosen or sir, causing Dewey to happily interjected, "Blue, if Av wants you to call him Av, then you're his best buddy too! Only his best buddies call him Av. That makes three, Av. You can only have one more."

Blue could only smile awkwardly. He wanted to oblige them both, but he considered it too definitive. Even though he expected his father to be imprisoned for some years, he still hoped for a miracle, and for the first time in his life, he felt lost.

Both boys felt awkward sharing the bed, so with the sheets pulled up to their necks, both looked upwards through the darkness.

"Blue?" Dewey whispered.

"Yeah?" Blue whispered back.

"So selling drugs is bad? That's why your dad was arrested, right?"

Blue wasn't in the mood to talk, but he still forced himself to whisper, "Normally, yeah, but Frank just sells weed. Not anything hard, just weed. It's a plant, like tobacco. Grows natural like, and it's pretty harmless. It's illegal but harmless. Most dealers sells everythin', soft and hard."

"What's the difference between soft and hard?"

"Some drugs can really mess ya up... and not only that, ya can get hooked. The Thirteenth Tribe pushes those."

"The Thirteenth Tribe?"

"Yeah, the motorcycle gang who wears the leather vests with all the patches. Ya must've seen 'em driving down Herring Cove Road. Their clubhouse is a few miles further down. Those guys sells the hard stuff. Some drugs can really zonk ya out, and others gives ya energy and makes ya all aggressive. Weed... weed just makes ya relaxed. It's not addictive, so Frank has no problem sellin' it. When 'is back's sore, sometimes 'e even smokes it. It makes 'im feel better... but stupid and forgetful too. He says weed is weaker than beer. No one gets aggressive with weed. No one fights, and there's hardly much of a hangover... a headache the next day. Mostly they laughs or gets all *philisophrical* and everythin'. Weed is strange. It can make ya hungry too... and makes everythin' tastes better. Frank tolds me 'e thinks things was invented with weed, like Clamato Juice." Blue imitated his father's slight French accent as he said, "Who but someone on weed would've come up with mixing clams with tomato juice?"

"You ever try it?"

"Clamato juice?" Blue joked.

Dewey laughed. "Yeah, Clamato Juice."

"Yeah. It tastes gross. They makes Caesars with it. "

"What's a Caesar?"

"It's a drink with booze."

"So, it's like a henway?"

Blue turned his head to Dewey. "A what?"

"A henway. You know... a henway," Dewey said as he tried not to laugh.

"No, what's a henway?"

"About six pounds as an adult," Dewey laughed.

Smiling, Blue turned back to stare upwards. "Ya been savin' that for a while, were ya?"

"Yup. Av got me with it last summer." Then, going back to his original question, he asked, "Seriously, you ever try the weed?"

"Yeah, once. It messed up my head, and I puked like you with your first cigarette there. And when Frank saw me, 'e knew right away and gave me shit. It does somethin' ta the eyes that shows ya smoked it. I never tried it since. Oh, and the smell, it smells strange. Not good, but not too bad. It's hard ta describe... sorta like a weak skunk smell."

"How long do you think he's going to be in jail for?"

"Ya tryin' ta get rid a me already?" Blue joked.

"No, just wondering," Dewey said, embarrassed for having asked.

"He could be there for a long time, maybe years. He'd prob'ly get let go if 'e'd give up his supplier, but 'e won't do that... and told me never ever ta do that, never."

"If you know who it is, then why not tell?"

Annoyed with the questions, Blue forced himself to say, "It's a respect thing. If 'e told, he'd be a rat and prob'ly gets in more troubles than 'e's in now, and if I told the cops, everyone'll thinks 'e did." Blue pause for a moment. "It's so crazy. The timin' is so crazy. He was thinkin' of quittin'. He said he made enough money. Oh, and..." Blue nudged Dewey with his elbow, "...and he has a big crush on yer mom and didn't want 'er to knows about the weed.

"It was startin' ta get scary, too. He was gettin' a lot of pressure from the Tribe to sell the harder stuff and no one says no ta 'em withouts gettin' in trouble, no one. He only gots away with it 'cause they likes 'im. One time, Tim bugged 'im ta do what they wanted, and 'e just teared in ta 'im. It was the only time I ever heard Frank yell and swear like a sailor. Even when I'm in trouble, 'e never yells. Anyway... that's all over now. We better try gettin' some sleep," Blue said, rolling away from Dewey. "Goodnight, Dwight."

"Goodnight, Blue."

With Dewey rolling away from Blue, both boys closed their eyes.

Then after a minute, Dewey opened his. "Hey, Blue?"

"Yeah?" Blue asked, annoyed.

"I'm glad you're here. It'll be like having a real brother."

"I'm glad too. Now go to sleep."

"Okay."

A minute later, Dewey said, "Blue? Blue? Hey, Blue."

"What!?"

"What about us getting the killer? Are we... are we still going to do that?"

"Huh? Why? They found 'im. It was Tim. He's dead. He... he killed 'imself. Goodnight, Dwight!"

"Seriously? Tim? And he's dead?" Dwight asked, rolling onto his back.

"Doesn't no one tell you nothin'? Yeah, it's all over. We'll talk about it later. Goodnight!"

Shocked, Dewey said, "Goodnight."

Dewey thought it strange how death was so common around him. In less than a year, he had four people he knew die, and all for different reasons: Mrs. Rosen from a heart attack, his dad from an accident, Stevie murdered, and now Tim by suicide. He also thought it strange that out of all those deaths, he felt almost nothing about Tim's death. Then relieved he wouldn't be acting as bait to catch the killer, but with questions popping into his head about Tim both killing himself and being the killer, he forced himself to think about something else.

"Blue?"

"What now, man!?"

"Whatever happened with Sally?"

"It never worked out."

"Why?"

"A religion thing."

"Seriously?"

"Yeah. Her parents wouldn't let us be together unless I was a Jehovah's Witness."

"That's not right."

"Yeah, her sister told on us. I'm starting ta thinks I'm followed by a dark cloud. If God's real, he must be testin' me."

"You still have me, you know."

"Yeah, I do," Blue said. "Goodnight, Dwight."

"Goodnight, Blue."

"Now try to sleep, okay?"

"Okay."

Then lying on his side again but with his eyes still opened, Dewey grinned. "Blue? Hey, Blue."

"Come on! Jesus! What now!?"

"Can you read me a bedtime story?" Dewey asked, before

roaring with laughter.

Blue kicked behind him, hitting Dewey's leg and causing him to roar with more laughter.

CHAPTER 16
Stress and Distraction

Blue didn't sleep well that Friday night. Being his first time with a bedmate and with the stress of his situation, he had a difficult time falling into a deep sleep, and it seemed to the little man he had only fallen asleep two hours before Dewey woke him by calling the bathroom first, which Blue appreciated since it would give him time to get his head on straight before breakfast.

Besides being tired, Blue had woken anxious, an almost unfamiliar feeling for him. He was worried. He worried that he was responsible for his father's arrest. Sure, his action most likely saved some lives, but the cost was Frank's imprisonment. Could anything he had done differently have avoided the search? If he had turned Tim in, would the police still have searched his place? But then, he felt, as soon as he entered the woods that afternoon, he was forced to do what he had done. If he didn't, he could've been killed. But could he have avoided everything by locking himself in the apartment and calling his father? He couldn't call the police, so calling Frank was the only option, and there was no doubt in his mind that his father would've acted in the extreme. Before Tim's death, he had never considered that his father could kill another man, but he also had never considered his father being so close to a man like Tim, a pedophile and a killer. Frank would normally have never let the past acts of a person bother him, like a man killing out of passion or killing by accident, but Blue expected that had his father known of a man molesting and/or killing children, he would react in the extreme, whether or not he was close to that man. Then with his mind all over the place, Blue again ponder the what-ifs: what if he didn't go into the woods; what if, instead, he had told Frank about Tim; what if Frank did take the law into his own hands; what if Frank was arrested for doing it, or... what if he had told Frank that he had killed Tim with Frank's gun?

He would eventually realize that nothing would come out of questioning his actions, since he couldn't reverse time, and he would have to accept things as they were.

During that Saturday morning's breakfast, Blue continued to address Lisa as Mrs. Dixon, except once when he made what he considered a faux pas. It was after breakfast and after several times of hearing Dewey call Lisa *Mom*, Blue thanked her for the breakfast by saying, "Thanks, Mom."

Dewey laughed, Lisa giggled, and Blue blushed.

It was the first time Dewey had seen his confident friend blush, and when he pointed it out, Blue said, "That bruise is goin' ta last ya a while."

"What bruise?"

"The one I'm goin' ta give ya."

Dewey laughed louder, and Blue broke a smirk.

A little later that morning, as Lisa prepared to go to work, Avriel showed up. After driving Lisa to work, he continued on downtown with Dewy and Blue sharing the passenger side of the front bench seat. The three visited the Nova Scotia Museum. They visited the stores along Quinpool Road, including the Candy Bowl, where they left with several small bags of sweets, and they took in a matinee. At six, they picked Lisa up from work and returned to downtown for supper at an Italian restaurant. They finished the day with bowling at the lower level of Eaton's Mall, just across the street from the Simpsons Mall.

Dewey had never bowled before and always wanted to try it, but he wanted to try the kind of bowling Fred Flintstone did, the sort with the holes in the balls, not the bowling they did with the smaller balls rolled at the stubby almost beer bottle-shaped pins that Blue told him were common in the city.

That day, Avriel came to realize that the boys didn't care so much about where they were. They cared more about carrying on together, cared more about being together.

Twice during their time downtown, as they were leaving one place to go to another, he noticed Detective Greene sitting in his parked car, looking everywhere but at them. He thought it a strange coincidence, but just a coincidence.

The next day, with Blue again tired from his lack of sleep the night before, Avriel again showed up after their breakfast to surprise Dewey and him with a bulging photo album. Almost a week before, Avriel had taken from the top of Dewey's dresser a pile of loose photos and two rolls of exposed film, and the night before, with the rolls developed, he had put together the album.

As Lisa, Blue, and Avriel looked on, Dewey opened the album to reveal on the first page a large photo of Stevie with his bright eyes and large smile. On the second page was a photo of all three boys sitting close together with the forest behind them. Dewey had taken the picture while holding the camera away from them and had cut off a portion of his face. Next, there were photos of the boys at the playground, hanging out at the Roi des Arbres, and in front of the Green Gables store with Blue and Stevie showing off their free bags of chips. There were photos of the three friends at Lisa's apartment and others of them at Frank's. The photos in the last third of the album were an assortment of pictures of Lisa, some posing and others protesting being photographed, and some of Avriel or Frank with and without the boys. The album ended with photos of Dewey's father.

After Avriel presented Blue with his own rectangular 110 camera and several rolls of film, which a surprised Blue humbly accepted, he told the boys that anyone who mattered to them would eventually end up in their photo albums and them in theirs. If there were no pictures of them, they probably weren't very important to them.

Like the previous day, the four also spent that Sunday out. With Dewey and Blue bringing their cameras, they went downtown and walked along the old harbor front, where they were permitted to board the Bluenose II, a fishing/racing schooner, *click, click, click*. They took the ferry to and from Dartmouth on the other side of the harbor, *click, click*. They enjoyed another matinee on Barrington Street, *click*, "Blue, not in here, please." They ate supper two blocks further down at a Chinese restaurant called The Canadiana, which reminded Avriel of a fifties diner, *click, click... click*. And they ended the night by taking in another movie at the Oxford Cinema, a romance that Lisa had chosen. While the boys quietly carried on through the movie, Lisa had to nudge Avriel awake several times when he began snoring so loudly that it caused some men in the cinema to laugh.

Leaving the cinema, Avriel almost thought he was seeing things when the four passed Detective Greene sitting in his parked car on the side of Barrington Street, and Blue confirmed the sighting when he joked, "Hey, I just saw the detective back there. He must be following us."

CHAPTER 17
Forgiveness over Permission

Passing Lisa and Dewey as they walked toward the boy's school, he hoped they didn't notice his car that easily stood out in that section of Herring Cove Road. Normally, he wouldn't be driving there until noon to pick Dewey up for lunch, but that day he was on a mission. Bunk beds were arriving that morning and he wanted to put them together before Lisa arrived home from work and refused them. Following the adage that it's better to ask for forgiveness than to ask for permission, he was confident that once he had assembled them, she would have to accept them. She wouldn't want him to go through the work of dissembling them and sending them back — after all, he was an old man.

Cautious of the barking dog in Mrs. Publicover's apartment, Sam followed behind Avriel as he lugged his old but pristine toolbox down the hallway and into Lisa's apartment where he set it down in Dewey's room. Removing the comforter and sheets from the boy's bed, he dropped them in a corner before lifting off the mattress and box spring, and with Sam supervising from the room's entrance, the old man took out a couple of tools and began disassembling the bed frame.

Impressed with his speed, he took three trips to Frank's

apartment, hauling down the box spring, the mattress, and the bed frame to place them up against the wall in Frank's hallway, and as he was leaving the apartment, he glanced into the living room and noticed more of a mess than the day before, when he and the boys had moved Blue's dresser to Dewey's already cramped room. Frank's sofa and chairs were flipped over, revealing the torn cloth lining of their bottoms. The back of the television was hanging off. The cases of the record and eight-track tape players were removed, and in the kitchen, the fridge and stove had been pulled away from the wall and the cabinet drawers were pulled out and emptied onto the floor. He guessed the police must have returned for a more thorough search, and then curious, he walked into Blue's room. The mattress was off the bed and sliced open and the dresser was pulled out from the wall and its drawers were on the floor, and in Frank's room, the drawers of his dresser were emptied on the floor and his mattress was also cut open.

Back in Lisa's apartment with Sam sleeping on his lap, he sat on the sofa impatiently waiting for the Sears delivery truck. After trying to read but finding the excitement of his mission blocking his ability to focus on the book, causing him to read several pages twice, he laid down *The Hobbit,* gently moved Sam from his lap, and stood up to stretch his back. Then after topping off the food and water in Sam's tray and cleaning the kitty litter, he took the garbage bag resting next to the door to the garbage room, and when he reached the putrid-smelling room, he remembered the garbage bag was full of clothes that Dewey had outgrown and that Lisa had cleared out of the closet and dresser to make room for Blue's. Knowing she planned to give them to the Salvation Army, Avriel took the bag to his car to drop off in the afternoon.

Ten minutes later, the delivery men announced their arrival via the door buzzer, and soon after that, Avriel was staring at two single mattresses covered in clear plastic, two long but narrow rectangular boxes, each containing an unassembled bunk bed, and a smaller rectangular box containing the ladder and side rails for the top bunk.

He dragged a box into Dewey's bedroom, and with an excitement that was rare for him, opened it and removed its many pieces. Then with his reading glasses on, he read the instructions and thought they were easy enough to put together, and they were until it appeared the holes on a wooden rail were misaligned by the manufacturer, but once Avriel realized he had placed the part on in reverse, he was soon finished assembling both bunks.

After adding the side railings to the second bunk bed and assembling the ladder, Avriel softly hammered wooden dowels into the holes drilled into the top of the first bunk's four bedposts and then thankful that they were made of light pinewood, carefully lifted the second bunk on top of the other, matching the dowels of the bottom bunk to the holes drilled into the bottom of the top bunk's posts. Satisfied, he used his palm to beat each post down onto the dowels. With holes for dowels drilled into the tops of the second bunk's posts too, making the beds identical, Avriel realized that even more beds could be stacked up and wondered how high they could safely go, and then realizing he was being silly, he screwed in the ladder. It was only when he set each mattress in place and pushed the bunk beds against the wall that he realized he had forgotten something rather important. Lisa would only have double and queen-sized sheets, so he would have to purchase sheets and blankets for the single beds.

Wiping the sweat from his brow, he put his glasses back on to look at his watch. It was almost eleven-thirty! What he thought had only taken minutes had taken him hours. Placing his glasses on the top bunk, Avriel grabbed the bundle of sheets he had earlier removed from Dewey's old bed, grabbed the detergent from the bathroom's narrow closet, and checked how many quarters he had with him. After wishing Sam a good afternoon, he left and locked the apartment door.

Twenty minutes later, he picked up Dewey from school and they hurried back to intercept Blue halfway down Autumn Drive to take him with them to MacDonald's.

While Avriel drove Dewey and Blue back to their schools, Blue asked if he could be back at Lisa's around five. He wanted to meet a friend after school, and Dewey knew exactly whom he was going to meet and figured he would probably meet her at the playground to let her know what was going on.

After dropping Blue off at school, Avriel was off to buy pillows, blankets, pillowcases, and sheets, and remembering his wife saying that one could never have enough of them, he made a mental note to buy several sets.

It was just past two-thirty when Avriel, with his arms full of plastic bags, made his way down the flight of stairs to the first floor, where a man in his early fifties was knocking on Frank's apartment door. As he passed the man, Avriel said over the barking of a small dog, "There is nobody home."

"Yeah, that's what I figured," the man said as he turned to see Avriel walking down the hall. Following him, he asked, "Do you know Frank? Do you know what's happening to his apartment?"

"I only met him once or twice," Avriel replied before sniffing the air and then sniffing it again to confirm it.

"I'm the landlord here. I own the building," the man said, almost having to shout over the barking.

"Right," Avriel said, laying the bags down at the apartment door, and after searching his pocket for its key, opened the door and dragged the bags to the entrance closet.

"Are you a relative of Mrs. Dixon?"

"Something like that."

"I'm Mr. Cawland... and you are?"

"A friend of the Dixons," Avriel said, having to fight the urge to close the door on the man.

"Okay. Uh... do you... does she happen to know if Frank'll be coming back soon? I've got to decide what to do about the apartment. If next month's rent isn't paid, I'll have to clear out his things and rent it."

"How much is the rent?"

"Two-twenty... a month."

"Right. Just a moment, please."

Avriel left the man standing at the door while he pulled out his checkbook from his spring jacket and walked into the kitchen.

"Who do I make the checks out to?" he asked, setting his checkbook on the counter.

"Uh... Cawland Enterprises. That's C-A-W-L-A-N-D Enterprises."

After a minute, Avriel met Mr. Cawland at the door. "Here are three postdated checks. We should know what is happening before you need more."

"Well, that's very kind of you, considering you only met Frank once or twice."

"I'm not doing it for Frank."

The man examined the checks. "Rosen, eh? That's Jewish, eh?"

"Yes."

"That's quite generous of you... for a Jew, I mean."

"Is that right?" Avriel asked, as he again fought to control his desire to close the door on the man. "You know many Jews that are strict with their money, do you?"

"Well... no... I was trying to pay you a compliment," the landlord said shyly.

"Try harder." Then about to close the door, he hesitated and said, "Now that we have taken care of Blue's... Frank's apartment, your next concern should probably be Mrs. Publicover's."

"Huh, why's that?"

"Do you smell that?"

The man sniffed the air. "The garbage room?"

"No, that is Mrs. Publicover," Avriel said and closed the door on the confused man.

Dewey was excited about the long-term implication of the beds, but Blue wasn't. He was thankful to have his own bed but hoped he wouldn't need it long. He had been treating his stay with the Dixons as a sleepover, an extended sleepover.

When Lisa returned home, she thanked a relieved Avriel with a hug and held back her giggle when she discovered he had bought six sets of sheets and pillowcases, as if he was preparing for more bunk beds in the future.

CHAPTER 18
Fitting In

Over the next few days, Blue became accustomed to calling Lisa and Avriel by their names, and just as two people forced together could become closer, Dewey and Blue became closer, though at times it might appear to be the opposite case. Each morning, the two squabbled over who would get to use the bathroom first, and twice it turned into a race that then turned into a wrestling match in the hallway with both equally motivated to win. Being more relaxed at the Dixons', Blue usually woke with a need for a number two, and Dewey dreaded being in the bathroom immediately after he satisfied it.

That following Friday evening, with Avriel and the two boys wearing black suits while Lisa wore a pink sleeveless dress, the four went out to celebrate her birthday.

Dewey was the most impressed by the restaurant and was glad to have brought his camera. The restaurant was almost the exact opposite of the one Avriel had brought him and his mother to the spring before. Where the previous restaurant was dark and gloomy, this new one was bright and lively, and as soon as they entered the reception area, they heard loud chatter and laughter before being impressed with the decor.

Next to the hostess station, a giant wide but narrow aquarium stood almost to the ceiling, and in it were large, colorful fish that Dewey had never seen before — there wasn't one goldfish in the bunch — and at the bottom were live plants that the fish took quick nibbles from, *click, click*. Everything in the restaurant seemed to be made of wood and glass, and the small lights embedded in the ceiling caused the glass to shine about as the hostess walked the group to their table where a spotless sheet of glass rested on top of a spotless white tablecloth, *click*. Dividing the dining room in half, putting every table in the restaurant against a wall, was a wood and glass barrier ending a foot from the ceiling, and behind the chairs separating the tables from one another was a section of dark-stained lattes six feet tall and half covered by vines growing up from a rectangular wooden pot at the bottom. And then there was their friendly waiter, dressed smartly in what Avriel explained to Dewey was a tuxedo, who impressed the boy so much that he thought he might want to be a waiter when he grew up. *click*.

At their table, as the others removed their jackets and placed their gifts on the extra chair their waiter had brought over for them, Lisa rubbed her shoulders to warm up from the short walk from the car, and while they looked at the menus, Blue, who was almost as impressed with the restaurant as Dewey, mentioned that the waiters' tuxedos were a little over the top. "They shouldn't be dressin' better than the customers," he told the others. "They won't get much tips that way. Who wants ta give money ta someone better dressed than 'em?"

Impressed with the boy's observation, Avriel broke a smile. "That is a good point, a very good point."

"Unless they adds it ta the bill like the French do," Blue added.

"They wouldn't do that," Dewey said.

"Sure, they might, and I'll bets ya yer dessert they does."

Avriel cut in. "Dewey, before you take that bet, do you want to risk your dessert over something so trivial?"

"I'll order two desserts then. You're on, Blue!"

"You'll order only one," Lisa told him.

Blue smiled. "Okay, after the desserts come, we ask the waiter about it."

When they finished their meal, they delayed ordering their desserts to give Lisa her presents. Dewey went first and gave her a small box wrapped in silver paper, which she unwrapped and was surprised to find a pair of silver earrings in the shape of stars. Next was Blue, who gave her a larger box wrapped in the same silver paper, and inside it, she found a carving of a dolphin diving out of water. And last was Avriel's gift of an envelope, which confused her until she looked inside and found several gift certificates from a hair and nail salon.

"Av, are you trying to tell me something?" Lisa joked.

"Yes," Avriel answered. "You work so hard that you deserve to treat yourself. They give massages also, a shoulder massage, that is. They told me a person gives it while they do your toenails."

"That sounds great!" Lisa smiled. "And it's for pedicures too!"

"Well, no. It's just for people. Sick pets have to go to the vet. I don't think they allow pets in there," Avriel said, smiling in his mind.

Lisa's smile was the only satisfaction he would get from the bad joke. When he looked at Blue and Dewey, they were just sitting there listening, so Avriel told himself it wasn't his joke, but that the boys were too short to catch it as it flew over their heads.

After finishing his *two* desserts, Blue excused himself to go to the bathroom. He had asked Dewey if he wanted to go with him, but at that moment, Dewey didn't want to go anywhere with his friend, who had eaten the desserts while repeating over and over how good they tasted. As Blue made his way to the bathroom at the far corner of the restaurant, he just barely recognized Art sitting at a table with a woman.

"Hey, Art. How's it goin'?"

Slightly startled, Art said, "Hey! Fancy... fancy meetin' ya 'ere! Nice suit, Blue. Who ya with?"

"Thanks, yers is nice too. I almost didn't recognize ya. I'm with Dwight and his folks. It's his mom's birthday. That's who I bought yer carvin' fer, remember?"

"My carvin'? Uh... right... cool. This 'ere's Alice. Alice, this is Blue. He lives in the same buildin' as me."

The thin brunette smiled. "Hi, Blue."

"Hello, Alice."

"Ya goin' ta the john?" Art asked, and when Blue nodded, he said, "Great, I have ta goes too."

Art picked up his cloth napkin from his lap and placed it on the table next to his empty plate. "Alice, nature calls. I'll be back in a sec."

Facing opposite walls, both flushed their urinals, zipped their flies, and made their way to the sinks.

"Hey, what do ya say we gets together fer some small game huntin' tomorrow afternoon? We haven't done it in a while, eh?"

Blue thought for a second. "Yeah, that sounds good. What time?"

"Two, or a little after. Hey, Alice doesn't like that I does it, so don't mentions it ta 'er, okay?"

"Sure. I didn't even knows ya had a girlfriend."

"She's new, almost three weeks. So come knockin' at two

then?" With Blue nodding, Art held the door open for him. "How long ya stayin' with Dwight?"

"Not sure. It could be a while," Blue reluctantly admitted.

"Hey, if it doesn't work out, ya have a sofa at my place anytime ya needs 'er, fer as longs as ya needs 'er."

Blue said only, "Okay." The offer surprised him, but he was more surprised that the offer was only for the sofa. Art lived in a two-bedroom apartment and when the boy had first visited Art's place to look at the new tenant's collection of wood carvings, Art told him the extra bedroom was for visitors. "Ya never know when a friend's goin' ta shows up fer a place ta stay."

When Art took his seat across from his girlfriend, Blue wished them a good evening and made his way back to his table.

Arriving back at the apartment building almost forty minutes later, Blue was surprised to see Art then in jeans and a spring jacket sweeping up his wood chips from around the cement steps, and by the pile of chips, it look like he had been there for a while.

"Man, yer fast!"

"Uh... yeah... Speedy Gonzales 'ere," Art said with a confused expression. "I... I figures I better cleans up before Cawland complains again," and as he leaned down to brush the chips into a dustpan, added, "Ya folks have a goodnight now."

After the four wished him a good evening, Lisa said, "Art, the dolphin you carved is beautiful."

"Oh, yeah?" Art asked, both surprised and flattered. "Thanks. So ya gots 'er tonight, then?" And when Lisa nodded with a smile, he said, "Then happy birthday."

"So tomorrow at two, right?" Blue asked.

"Huh? Oh... rights... yeah, tomorrow at two... sure."

Entering the building, Blue whispered to the three, "That man has a serious memory problem! I already told 'im at the restaurant I gave ya the carvin', and it was 'is idea ta meet up tomorrow!"

CHAPTER 19
Hobby and Hunting

Straining to carry the plastic bag that was straining to hold a half-gallon plastic bottle of pop that had grown heavier during the walk from the store, Dewey met Art at the steps of their apartment building as he was preparing to carve something from a rectangular block of wood.

"Hi, Art," Dewey said. "Blue's back?"

"Hey, Dwight. Blue? I don't knows where 'e is."

"Wasn't he hunting with you? He told me he was going to."

"Yeah, that's true. S'posed ta, but he tolds me 'e had other plans."

"Other plans? He didn't tell me. I thought he left at two to go to your place."

"Oh, yeah? Maybe it was that girl. You know the girl he likes," Art said, as he began cutting away at the wood.

"Sally? But they broke up."

"Sally, right, that's it," he said, continuing to cut pieces from the wood. "Maybe they worked it out, or somethin'. Alls I knows is 'e had other plans." Art stopped carving. "That's all I cans tell ya. I guess yer takin' home the... what is that, Sprite?"

"Yup, we're having Chinese. They didn't have Sprite at

the restaurant and Mom won't let us drink Coke at night. She says it's not good at nighttime."

"Chinese is good. Hey, are ya goin' to ask me what I'm carvin'. Come on, ask me. Ya haven't asked, and ya always ask, eh?"

"Okay," Dewey smiled awkwardly. "What are you carving?"

"A train, an early one. The kind they threw coal inta."

"Cool."

"No, coal," the man laughed. "Hey... uh... ya wants ta learn ta carve too? I'll teach ya. It's real easy. It just takes patience, lots of 'er."

"Sure, I guess. I have a knife."

"Ya gots a knife?"

"Yup, seriously." Dewey laid the bag down on the concrete steps and pulled the small pocketknife from his front pocket. "I got it as a... a prize."

"Prize? What fer?"

"Uh... singing."

Art took the knife and pulled out its blade. "That's a good one. Yer halfway there now, eh? We can gets ya ready now fer whens ya start," he said as he closed the blade and handed it back to Dewey.

"Seriously?"

"Sure. It'll take a few minutes ta finds ya some wood in the woods there, and while we're lookin', I'll tells ya the basics."

"Cool... but I should get home," Dewey said, feeling pulled in two directions.

"It'll only take a sec," he said, setting his block of wood aside and picking up the plastic bag. "We'll just keep this out of the sun and be back lickety-split." After he leaned over to place the bag and his block wood on the pavement in the shade of the cement steps, he closed his knife, placed it in his pocket, and stood up brushing away the few cuttings from his lap. "Who knows, maybe we'll even meets up with Blue and Sandy."

"Sally," Dewey corrected the man.

"Right, Sally. Wouldn't Blue just shits himself if we walks in on 'em kissin' it up!" he laughed. "Okay, let's go. We have ta hurry before yer pop there gets warm." With Dewey following him into the woods at the end of the street, he said, "Okay, first we gotta finds ya piece of wood based on what yer gonna carve. So whats ya wants ta carve? Think simple fer yer first."

"I don't know. I'll have to think about it," Dewey said as he tried to keep up with the man while watching where he stepped.

"I started with a turtle. There's no thin or small parts on 'em, just the round shell and six thick things stickin' out."

"Okay, I'll carve that," Dewey said, getting excited about it.

"Right, then keep yer eyes out fer a piece a wood that's abouts four inches square and abouts two inches thick. Any bigger and ya'll be carvin' forever."

"But don't you use wood that's already cut, and how do we find a square piece of wood in the woods?"

"Right... I do... but... but we can find a good size piece here, and I can... I can cut 'er with a saw fer ya."

"Okay," Dewey said, only then feeling apprehensive about the project when it occurred to him how his mother would feel about it. If she knew about it, she would know about the knife, and he was certain she wouldn't approve of it. But then he expected that if he kept it a secret until he gave her the carved turtle, she would have a hard time denying him the hobby after he had impressed her with it. And she would have to like a turtle. Everyone likes turtles. They were like dolphins, and she loved the dolphin Blue had given her.

After Art told him there were no good pieces at the edge of it, they walked further into the woods as he gave Dewey tips. "Always cut aways from ya and work slow like. The faster ya carves, the more mistakes ya'll makes and more chances a cuttin' yerself. I ruined my first turtle tryin' ta rush the legs. One came right off. Ya have ta cuts slow like, slow on purpose fer a purpose. We'll has ta gets ya some sandpaper ta smooth it all outs when yer finished. Now the trick ta carvin' is bein' able ta see the carvin' in the wood before ya even starts." As they made their way further into the woods, all Dewey saw on the ground were thin branches and thick rotting ones, and as if reading his mind, Art said, "So we has ta find wood that's dry but not rottin'. There's nothing 'ere, so it looks like we'll has ta look deeper in the woods there."

"Do we need any special kind of wood? I think there's only maple and pine trees here."

"Good question. Yer a bright kid. Nope, anythin's good. We just gots ta find us a short piece of thick branch. If we cuts branches off, ya'd have ta wait a while fer 'em ta dry. If we finds a thick, broken branch, ya can start yer carvin' tonight."

While trying to keep up with his carving instructor, Dewey continued to search the ground for large pieces of broken branches, paying no attention to where they were going until they forced themselves through a dense patch of younger trees, where he was surprised to find they were standing in a clearing. "Hey, I know this place. This is Roi des Arbres... because of that giant tree th—" Dewey's jaw dropped.

**

That day, Avriel learned that Chinese food smells good in a small dose, but when the smell took over the apartment, it took away his appetite, and after opening the windows of both the living/dining room and kitchen, placing the bags of food in the oven to keep them warm, and then scooping up Sam, he left the apartment to sit on the steps with Sam on his lap, both appreciating the cool breeze.

Five minutes earlier, Avriel had wondered what was taking Dewey so long to return from the store, but now it turned into worry, a worry that also included Blue, who was supposed to be back half an hour ago.

Just as it occurred to Avriel that the boys had probably met up with each other along Herring Cove Road and got sidetracked, Sam turned his head toward the woods and his ears twisted forward. Making a short meow, he stood up and jumped off Avriel's lap.

"Where are you going?" Avriel asked, as if Sam would reply.

Stopping, Sam looked back at Avriel for a second before continuing toward the woods.

Worried that he might have to chase after his cat, Avriel descended the cement steps and spotted the plastic bag holding the bottle of Sprite and tried to make sense of it and the block of partially carved wood beside it. Then a smell hit his nostrils. Not the mild perfume he would've expected, but the pungent smell of death, but when he cautiously sniffed the air to confirm it, there was nothing.

With the old man's heart racing, he looked toward the woods where Sam had disappeared, and calling out to him, he hurried through the trees, ignoring the branches' many successful attempts to snag him. After a few seconds, he stopped and called out to Sam again. Hearing a meow ahead of him, he also heard muffled shouts. He couldn't make out what was being shouted, but he was certain they were shouting. Then, after rushing ahead for a minute, he stopped again to call out to Sam, and again Sam responded with a meow, but the shouts were gone.

As he made his way toward the cat's last response, Avriel ignored the sweat mixing with the blood trickling down from the scratches on his forehead. He ignored the pains in his legs as they strained to continue to do as he demanded, and he ignored the branches of the trees snagging his shirt and pants as they tried to prevent him from passing through to the clearing ahead.

Breaking through, he stood frozen as he tried to make sense of what he was seeing.

**

Sitting against a large tree, Art pulled down a branch from above him, shook it, and watched a few pine needles fall on him. "How's yer arm? That constant breakin' ta loads the pellets must be takin' a toll on 'er. Too bad there's no semi-automatic ones out there, eh? Just load a bunch and then just starts pullin' the trigger. Wouldn't that be great, eh?"

"That'd be easier. They gots 'em for BB guns but not for pellet guns," Blue said as he sat next to him against the tree.

"Yeah, but BB guns have no power. They can't even put a hole in a tin can. Maybe we'll look at gettin' a twenty-two fer ya. Hey, speakin' a tin cans, could ya grabs two Cokes?"

Blue picked up the knapsack resting on top of a pellet gun, a bow, and a tube of metal-tipped arrows. "But wouldn't I need a huntin' license for that?"

"Nah, I won't tells if ya don't. It's quiet too. Just a loud crackin' sound, not much of a bang. Not like a thirty-eight. Now, they makes lots of noise, right?" Art said as he took a can of Coke from Blue and both cracked them open.

"Uh... I don't know anythin' abouts that. I never heard one."

"A thirty-eight has a big kick too," the man continued. "There's not much with a twenty-two. It's really just a step up from a pellet gun. Really, twenty-two handguns are girly guns. Ya get shot by one of 'em, ya usually lives ta talk about 'er, but a thirty-eight, nope. They have a hell of a kick too. Ya ever experience the kick of a thirty-eight?"

"No. If I never heard one, I prob'ly never fired one, right?"

"That's true... I guess."

As the two sat quietly drinking their Cokes for a minute, Blue watched him pick needles off the branch above him and thought his friend seemed to have something more on his mind.

Then brushing the needles from his lap, Art said, "I likes ya, Blue. Yer a pretty cool kid. My mom would'a called ya an old soul, mature fer yer age and all that. That's what she used ta call us, old souls. Yup, I've been all overs the place and never mets no one like ya."

"Okay," Blue said, feeling uncomfortable with where the conversation might be going. "We should gets goin'. If I'm not back by supper, Av's gonna start worryin'."

As Blue started to get up, Art pulled him back down. "Just a sec, bud. I didn't means ta sound weird there. I'm not a perv... not a perv like Tim, not a perv at all. I just likes ya as a bud, that's it. Give me a sec ta finish my Coke and we'll gets outta here." Art's words should've relaxed Blue but the pulling back down was strangely aggressive. "It was just back there where Tim was killed, ya knows," he said, pointing behind them in the opposite direction of Autumn Drive. "He was... he shots himself just back theres in a little clearin'. Maybe his ghost haunts this place now. Maybe he's wanderin' the woods lookin' fer revenge."

"Revenge?" the boy asked. "Why'd he need revenge? Who'd he have ta revenge?"

"Maybe you," Art said, causing Blue to drop his almost empty can of Coke and then pick it up. "I don't knows. I'm just talkin' shit, but ya should'a sees yer face just then!"

Annoyed, Blue looked at his watch. "Okay, let's go." He laid his can down, picked up the knapsack and pellet gun, and stood up out of the way of the tree's branches. "It's almost six-thirty. I've gotta get back."

"Sure. In a sec. First, I got somethin' fer ya." After reaching into his pocket, he held out two thirty-eight bullets. "Here, ya dropped these."

Blue's eyes widened. His heart beat hard, and his face almost matched the color of his hair.

"With all the commotion, ya missed them on the ground. Not sure whys ya wanted ta bring extra rounds when ya already had five or six of 'em loaded, but 'eres ya go. If the cops had got 'em, they might've gots yer fingerprints from 'em, eh?"

Frozen, Blue could only look down at Art.

"Go ahead and take 'em. Jesus, don't look so shocked. I see everythin' that goes on 'ere. It's like I gots me four eyes, and no, I'm not goin' ta say shit ta no one. It's are secret," he said before shaking the rounds in his palm. "So... ya wants the souvenirs or what?"

Blue shook his head nervously.

"Fine, I'll keeps 'em then. Don't worry. There's no way a trackin'em back to nobody. So, I'm guessin' you brought extras just ta shows the perv ya had 'em, prove the gun's loaded. Am I right?"

Blue nodded his head stiffly. His lips were dry and his heart was trying to escape his chest.

"I knew it! Damn, I love bein' right. Jesus, Blue, yer head's pourin' sweat. Relax, I already tolds ya it's cool. Now sit back down 'ere. Sits down and relax."

Almost robotically, Blue returned to where he was sitting and looked straight ahead, and when Art placed his hand on his knee, Blue reflexively slapped it away. Laughing, Art said, "Sorry, I couldn't resist messin' with ya! Yer wound tighter than the bow there! Jesus Christ, it's like talkin' ta a zombie, a stressed-out zombie. Look, I was goin' ta tells ya my secret... so we can have somethin' on each other. Ya wanna hears it?" After Blue shook his head, he said, "Well, I'll tells ya anyways. Tim didn't kills the kids, nope. He did God knows what ta 'em, but he never killed 'em. Ya did kill a sick freak though. There's no question there. No ones goin' ta argue with that, but ya didn't gun downs a killer... gun 'im down in cold blood. Jesus! Is this freakin' ya out or what? And I haven't even told ya my secret yet. But maybe ya already figured 'er out... bein' the smart guy that ya are, eh? Eh?" Art said, nudging Blue several times. "Ya knows what it is, do ya?" With Blue saying nothing, he grinned. "Come on, ya knows what it is? No? Really?" Art pulled a lighter and a pack of cigarettes from his jacket pocket, placed a cigarette between his lips, and lit it. After taking a long drag from it, he offered it to Blue, who shook his head. "Okay, here goes. Get ready for it. It's me. I killed 'em kids."

Blue's eyes widened as he turned his head to Art and forced out a whisper. "Ya... ya killed Stevie?"

"Yes... well no. I didn't kills 'im or even all a the kids, but I knows who did," Art said before his voice took a sympathetic tone. "I know 'e was yer friend and all, but 'e'd've grown ups a burden on society. He coulds hardly speak and was dumb as a doornail. Really, his death saves society from a future burden. Hell, it saves it from a burden now. That's why I does it. I get rid of the burdens. Okay, I admits it, I really gets off on killin' small things, includin' kids, but if ya think abouts it, no one really cares anyway. A child goes missin'ere, and the cops thinks it's run away. They don't go searchin' and ya never even hears about a missin' kid unless it's from a well-ta-do family." Art took a drag off the cigarette. "But now it's gettin' harder, with 'em findin' the bodies and all. That's why I wants ya ta join me. We can do it together. Ya lures 'em in and I does the killin'. Hell, we'll even do that together, eh? Ya killed the perv, ya can kills others, right? Sure, ya killed because ya justified it ta yerself, but it's no different from what I does. Maybe those kids aren't that bad now, but they will be when they grows up. It's justified. Here, wet yer throat." Art handed his can of Coke to Blue, who didn't move, so he took the boy's hand and placed the can in it. "Now have a drink."

Blue put the can to his dry lips and took two gulps. It burned his throat, and just as it reached his stomach, he twisted to the side and vomited it back out.

"That's it. That should makes ya feels better. Now take another gulp and wipe yer chin."

Blue forced down more of the Coke, wiped his chin with the sleeve of his jacket, and then whispered in disbelief, "But how... how'd ya kill Stevie? Ya were at the buildin' when 'e left. I saw ya carvin'."

"I told ya I didn't kill 'im, but I knows who did. Okay, let's get out'a here." he crushed his cigarette into the dirt, grabbed his bow and case of arrows, and made his way out from under the tree's branches to stand up. "Come on, let's get goin'. I have somethin' else ta show ya befores yer supper." With Blue still sitting, he glared down at him. "Jesus! Ya won't sit and now ya won't stand! Pick up the bag and rifle and come on! Yer the one in a hurry, remember! Get up!" With shaking hands, Blue grabbed the knapsack and pellet gun and stood up. "There ya go. Now remembers when yer eatin' supper, I knows yer secret, so if ya tells, I tells. The great thing about the walk outta here is ya'll gets a chance ta get yer shit together. We don't want people noticin' and askin' questions do we... do we?" he asked as he placed the tube of arrows over a shoulder.

As Blue shook his head while sliding the knapsack over a shoulder, both heard someone or something approaching from their left, and when Art poked through the wall of trees followed seconds later by Dewey, Blue didn't understand what he was seeing.

"Hey, I know this place!" Dewey said. "This is Roi des Arbres... because of that giant tree th—"

Dewey dropped his jaw just as Blue dropped the pellet gun and knapsack, and each looked to the Art beside them and then to the identically dressed Art across from them. Then the boys looked at each other.

Breaking through his confusion, Blue yelled, "DWIGHT, RUN! RUN!"

Stunned, Dewey continued to stand where he was as he repeatedly looked from Blue to Blue's Art.

"RUN! DWIGHT, RUN!"

"Oh, no you don't!" Dewey's Art said, grabbing him by his jacket and dragging him over to Blue and his Art.

"Blue, what's going on?" a watery-eyed Dewey asked.

"Yeah, *Roger*, what's goin' on?" Blue's Art asked. "Guys, this is Roger. Yas prob'ly guessed we're identical twins, but I'm the better lookin' one," he joked. "Roger, why the 'ells are ya bringin' that kid inta this fer? That wasn't the plan, was it?"

Obviously ashamed, Roger said, "I knows! I knows! But I met up with this little shit and 'is questions. I had no choice! Ya was takin' too longs ta kills 'im!"

"Kill 'im? That wasn't part of the plan!"

"I knows, but I figured the plan must'a changed when yas didn't shows up whens ya saids yas would, so I went outside for the alibi."

With his hand hanging down by his side, Blue gestured to Dewey with a subtle stabbing motion and had to do it twice before Dewey could clear his mind and figure out what his friend was asking for.

"Okay, so what now, Roger? Ya plannin' on killin' the kid, are ya? YA HAD YER TURN ALREADY!"

As Dewey slowly reached into his front pocket and pulled out his pocketknife, Roger's shame turned into anger, and he said, "Then ya do it! I mades this one easy fer ya, eh? No waitin' around fer this one, and ya gots plenty a time before the sun goes down. Yer very welcome, brother!"

When Dewey tried to hand the knife to Blue, Art pushed the redhead aside and grabbed it. "Did ya see that, Roger? Man, yer careless! You should'a took 'is knife!"

Roger's face reddened. "Idiot!" he hissed as he smacked the back of Dewey's head so hard that the boy fell forward and slammed into the soft ground where his head bounced before he rested unconscious facedown on the ground.

Tapping Dewey with his foot, Art asked, "What the 'ell am I s'posed to do with a knocked-out kid? Roger, can ya mess up any more today? Now we gotta wait until he wakes up before I can have my fun!" Then something occurred to him and he looked at Blue. "Hey, this can work out good. Blue, ya can have yer first kill. Ya ups for that?" Blue's eyes widened as he shook his head. "It'll be cool. I'll walks ya through it. The first is always the best rush. It'd be our fifteenth, so no biggy anymore fer us. Sure, we've only got four here... one they never found, but we've been all over the place doing this fer years now. We're pros ya know."

Blue wanted to run away, and he may have if Dewey wasn't lying there. Then he considered grabbing the pellet gun from the ground. A pellet wouldn't do much damage unless he shot one of them in the eye, but the rifle's butt could do some.

"Come on! Ya'll love it! It won't be like Tim, where ya just shoots 'em. Ya gets ta sees the fear and pain in 'is eyes.

That's the bestest thing abouts it!"

"Wait, so he gets ta do it? Really?" Roger complained, "Then I has ta waits fer ya ta kills another one befores I gets my turn again! That's gonna be months!"

"Stop yer whinin'! Ya can kills the next one," his brother hissed.

Then smiling, Roger said, "Okay, cool. So let's get the party goin' then."

"There ain't no party. Ya have ta go back and sits on the steps."

"Shit man, and miss all the fun?"

"We gotta cover are asses, eh? So—"

The sound of someone calling out for someone named Sam caught Art's attention.

"So? So what?" Roger asked. "Maybe, I can stay this time, and we uses Blue as are alibi."

When Art shot his finger up to his lips, Roger got the signal and grabbed Blue, wrapping an arm around his throat and placing a hand over his mouth.

They only had to wait seconds for Sam to enter the clearing, where he stopped and stared at the four.

Art whispered, "Don't anyone move."

As Blue struggled to get away from Roger, who tightened his grip, Art reached behind him and quickly pulled an arrow from the tube, placed it against the bow's string, and pulled back. He paused when he heard more rustling of branches before a confused Avriel stepped into the clearing.

With Roger preventing Blue from warning his older friend, Art smiled as he raised his bow at the old man.

Avriel felt something burn his right shoulder and then seconds later felt something bite into his thigh. With his legs giving out, he fell over onto his side. Trying to get up, the pain in his failing leg forced him to look down to see the arrow sticking out of his thigh. Then he noticed the arrow in his shoulder. Breathing heavily and becoming weak, he rolled onto his back and groaned as the portion of the arrow sticking out from the back of his shoulder bent under his weight.

Releasing his hold on Blue, Roger said with surprise, "Ya missed 'is heart! Twice ya missed 'im! Ya actually missed!"

"I didn't miss nothin'! I want Blue ta have time ta see 'im die. The shoulder shot there was just ta bring 'im down. That didn't do it, so I had ta goes fer a leg."

"See, that's why yer the smart one. Always thinkin'," Roger said with his face glowing with joy.

With Avriel groaning, Art ordered, "Get the cat there!"

Roger released Blue, slowly walked over to Sam, who was examining the arrow in Avriel's leg, and picked him up by the scruff of his neck.

"Okay, on three throw it up in the air," Art said as he grabbed and stretched back a third arrow. "One... two... three."

As Sam hissed and Roger tossed him straight up into the air, Art aimed his bow, but before he could release the arrow, Blue screamed "NO!" and landed a haymaker in his stomach, causing Art to bend forward.

Landing on all fours, Sam arched his back, hissed at Art, and took off into the woods.

Frozen, Roger looked down at the arrow sticking out of his chest, looked at Art, and said, "Brother?" before falling backward.

"WHAT THE HELL!?" Art yelled and looked over at Blue just in time to see the swing of the pellet gun. Blocking it with his bow, he slashed out with the end of it and caught the boy on the chin, sending him to the ground with a gash in it.

"STAY THERE, YA LITTLE SHIT! STAY THERE! I'M GOIN' TA KILLS YA AFTER MAKIN' YA WATCH ME KILLS THE OTHER SHIT THERE!"

Art walked over to his brother and looked down at him in disbelief. "SHIT! SHIT! SHIT!" Then with tears in his eyes, he shook as he looked back at Blue looking back at him from the ground. "Ya really messed up! I'm goin' ta makes yer death so painful ya'll be beggin' me ta kills ya! But first... first yer goin' to watch me finish this fucker off," Art said before he walked over to Avriel and reached down to pull the arrow from his thigh.

With Avriel groaning and grabbing weakly at his pant leg, Art said, "I guess I can't reuse that one." Straightening up, he pulled another from the tube and stretched it back on the string. "Ya watchin' this, ya little shit?" he said as he took two steps back.

Avriel looked over at Blue, forced out, "Blue, close your eyes," and then his eyes widened with fear.

Relaxing the tension on the bow to look back at what the old man was fearful of, Art saw Blue coming at him, ready to swing the butt of the rifle like a baseball bat.

Blue never got to follow through with the swing. He never heard the loud bang and never felt the pain from the impact that lifted him into the air and tossed him back several feet.

"What the hell?" were the last words Art said as three more blasts from a pistol behind him, stretched out through the wall of trees, sent him to the ground.

When he opened his eyes, it took him a few seconds to realize he had been knocked unconscious, and he realized too that Stevie was right when he once whispered to him, "When yer knocked out, ya doesn't feels it until ya wakes up." With his head hurting, everything came back to him and he began to panic. Sitting up, he looked around and saw Blue lying face down near one of the Arts, who was on his back with his arms and legs spread. He saw the other Art on his back with an arrow sticking straight up from his chest, and even stranger still, he saw Avriel on his back with two arrows sticking out of him and a man kneeling over him. Feeling like he had drunk several beers, he struggled to stand up and walk over to Avriel, but after a few steps, he stumbled and fell to the ground.

The man kneeling over Avriel spun around with his gun in hand and relaxed when he saw Dewey. Sliding his gun into his shoulder holster, the detective walked over to him and said, "It's going to be all right. It's all over now."

**

As the bus slowed to a stop, two ambulances sped toward it from the opposite direction, one right after the other, their lights flashing and their sirens screaming.

With her work shoes in a plastic bag, Lisa waited for the bus to leave before crossing the street, and in her excitement to tell everyone the news she received that morning, she almost skipped to Autumn Drive. Turning onto the gravel road, she stopped to stare down at the end of it where lights were flashing and a group of people was surrounding several vehicles. As an ambulance squeezed through the crowd and sped toward her, she dropped her bag, ran down the gravel road, and in seconds and with tears obstructing her vision and her heart racing, she reached the crowd where on the other side of it were three police cars and another ambulance.

She tried to scream, but nothing came out. She tried pushing through the crowd, but a police officer held her back. She tried to say something, but couldn't form the words.

"It's okay. She's the mother," Detective Greene told the officer as he walked over to her, and taking her arm, he gently walked her to the hood of a police car. "Mrs. Dixon, you should sit. There's been a... a situation."

The two paramedics coming out of the woods carrying a long and heavy black bag was the last thing she saw.

CHAPTER 20
Family

Parked near the side of a large Victorian-style home at the end of the long paved driveway, Av, in a black suit, sat behind the wheel of his Cadillac staring out at the large covered in-ground pool that appeared smaller when surrounded by the large and recently manicured backyard with its rock garden at the far back that included a stained wooden bridge over an empty stonewalled fishpond. As a stocky older man in overalls carrying a black-stained can of paint passed the car, the two exchanged waves and Avriel watched him walk over to a section of rusty iron fence at the far corner of the yard, lay down the can, take out a metal brush from his overalls, and start scraping at the rust and loose pieces of black paint.

Putting the car in reverse and straining his neck to look behind him, he slowly backed out from between a two-door Chevrolet Chevette and an old pickup. When he passed the house, he backed onto the branch of the driveway that went as far as the house's front double doors, put the car in park, and stared to his left at the large, recently mowed front lawn surrounded by an iron fence with its two iron gates opened at the driveway's entrance further down.

Occasionally, when he thought about it, he was amazed at the direction his life had taken. If anyone had predicted it would be as it was, he would've thought them crazy, but as it was, he was truly content that he was sharing his life with several people he loved, and even though he didn't like thinking about how his life would've been if his wife hadn't moved them to Gilmore Street, he expected it would've been unbearably lonely, a self-inflicted loneliness. He expected too that if she were looking down on them, she would be proud of him.

Av had spent just over three weeks at the hospital in a private room on the surgery recovery floor, and it fascinated him that his only two times in a hospital bed weren't because of an illness or an accident but because someone had tried to kill him, once during the war and once almost three months back. It fascinated him too how it was at a hospital where his relationship with Lisa and Dwight had begun, and it was during his recent stay there that his bond with Blue grew.

While Lisa and Dwight split their free time between visiting the two, Blue, who was at the children's hospital only a ten-minute walk away, snuck out during the days to visit Av for two or three hours. Several times the old man would wake up to find the little man reading one of the books Lisa had brought him, and they usually spent a portion of their time together discussing what Blue had read. During those visits, Av had developed a great fondness for Blue, but then how could he not when the boy risked his life to try and save him?

Avriel couldn't help but respect Blue's father for bringing him up well, and it was that respect that gave the introverted old man the courage to take Blue every Sunday afternoon to visit him in prison, but he still couldn't bring himself to like the man.

Lisa never allowed Dwight to go along with them, and she never went along either. She hadn't yet forgiven Frank for his poor choices in occupation and friends.

**

At one end of the wide hallway, two doors facing each other opened as if synchronized, and Dwight and Blue walked out of their bedrooms in their school uniforms of a pair of black dress pants, a white dress shirt, a black tie, and a black blazer to stare at each other for a second before exchanging thumbs-ups.

At the stairs dividing the long hallway, the two met a small woman, aged somewhere between Lisa and Av, coming up the floating stairs in what looked like green hospital scrubs.

"Hi, Mrs. Collins. Hi, Sam," they said.

"Good morning, gentlemen. Look at that, he's still behind me. I swear this cat is afraid I'm going to steal something. He hasn't left my side since I got here this morning, and he does this all the time."

"He's trying to get you to like him," Dwight said.

"Well, stalking me isn't going to do that."

"Hey, Mrs. Collins, ya might wants ta save my bathroom until last, if ya knows what I means," Blue warned her.

"I know what you mean, and I always do. Have a wonderful first day at school, you two."

As the woman made her way toward Dwight's bedroom, with Sam following her, both boys wished her a good day before Blue whispered to Dwight, "Race ya down the banisters."

"This time, I'm going to beat you," Dwight whispered back.

Each grabbed a banister, wrapped their bodies around it, slid down, and just before reaching the large ball at its end, Blue swung his body off of it to land on the marble floor of the foyer, but Dwight wasn't so elegant and only dismounted after groaning loudly from his backside hitting the ball.

"That's now three outta three," Blue grinned.

"Yeah, but only because of the ball!" Dwight protested.

"Are you two sliding down the banisters again?" Lisa asked from the kitchen.

"No," Dwight replied.

"Yes," Blue replied and then looked at Dwight and whispered, "Ya know how she knows? Yer *arrrggghhh.*"

"Is that bruise new?" Dwight asked.

"What bruise?"

"That one," Dwight said as he punched him in the shoulder and took off laughing.

Joining Lisa as she drank her coffee on a stool at the island in the middle of the large kitchen, the two put their arms out to their sides and exclaimed, "Tah-dah!"

"Dewey, you look so cute, and don't you look dashing, Blue!"

"It's Dwight, and I don't want to look cute! I want to look dashing too!"

"And you will when you're a little older," Lisa said.

"Like when yer forty," Blue added with a smirk, causing Dwight to punch him in the shoulder again.

"Boys, your lunches are on the counter by the fridge. Where are your book bags?"

"Upstairs," they said together.

"Really? Okay, grab your lunches and go get your bags. I think Av's more excited about your first day of school than you are. He's been waiting in the car since you ate breakfast. Now hurry and I'll see you at supper. My last class ends at six, so I'll be back from university by six-thirty." Then, watching the two grab their lunches and then leave to get their bags, she added, "And no more banister races. Please, don't make me worry."

"Okay, Mom," Dwight said. "Hey, Blue, that's something I'll never hear you say."

"What?"

"I'll be back from university," Dwight said, before laughing.

"Maybe, but I've a better chance of sayin' that than ya ever sayin' ya won somethin'."

The back door opened, and both boys threw in their school bags and slid onto the back seat. "To school, James," they said and then laughed at the joke they had planned a minute earlier.

Av missed what they said and was confused when both boys climbed over to the front seat, with Dwight satisfied to get the window.

Their old friend asked, "Do you two have everything? Lunches and—"

"Yup," Dwight said.

"Money? Do you need money?" he asked as he put the car in drive and drove to the main section of the driveway.

"I'm good. I still have money from my allowance," Blue said.

Av turned left onto Jubilee Drive. "Did you not just buy a model house for the train set?"

"Yup, but I'm good," Dwight grinned. "Blue still has money from his allowance."

Av reached into his pocket, pulled out a crumpled five-dollar bill, and handed it to Blue. "In case you fall short. I don't know what the prices are like at that school, but I expect nothing there is cheap."

"Thanks," Blue said, taking the bill and passing it to Dwight.

"So, are you two excited?"

"A bit nervous," admitted Dwight.

"Not so much," admitted Blue.

"Do you remember the only thing Lisa had asked of you?"

"Yup," Dwight jumped in. "No talking about the Kid

Killers and Blue can't show off his scar."

"Ding, ding, ding! The boy wins a prize."

"Seriously?"

"Yes, and Blue just gave it to you."

The drive to the school took less than five minutes, and after they passed through its gate, Av followed the line of cars dropping off kids.

"I guess you wore your suit for nothing," Dwight said. "The parents aren't going in with them."

Av put the car in park. "Right. I guess this is where we part, but one more question: what is the first thing you do when you go inside?"

"Find the biggest kid and start a fight with 'im," Blue said, causing Dwight to laugh.

Av smiled. "No. This isn't Spryfield."

"We find the smallest kid?" Blue continued with his joke.

"We find out where our homeroom is and go there."

"Ding, ding, ding! The boy wins a prize!"

"Seriously?"

"No. Now, you two have a great day, and when I pick you up at three-thirty, I want to hear all about it."

Wishing Av a good day, Dwight left the car with Blue about to follow.

"Uh, Blue, just one thing," Av said, causing Blue to sit back down and Dwight to wait for him at the far edge of the sidewalk as children walked past him. "Do you... do you remember when we first met, how you talked very well... very distinctly? You dropped much of your... your Maritime... Maritime English."

"Sure, yeah."

"Well, I expect here they all speak much the same way, without the Maritime English, I mean to say. I only say this out of concern for the way they may treat you if you use your normal way of speaking. When I first went to Cambridge, I had to adjust my way of speaking. I had to force myself to enunciate clearly. Everyone was expected to speak in the same manner. They called it Learned Pronunciation. Now, do not get me wrong, I have heard much stronger Maritime accents, but what I am trying to say is that if you speak here as you spoke when we first met, I expect you will be treated with more respect. I only say this because I know you are capable."

"Okay, I... I s'pose yer right. I mean, I *suppose* you're right. I can try. Does that mean I have to avoid conjugating, too?"

The old man smiled. "I think you mean contractions, and no, that is a... a habit I had picked up a while back."

"Okay, but then you have to start using conjug... contractions, and I bet I can last longer than you."

Then, surprised by the challenge that he was sure he would win, Av said, "Sure... we can do that. If we, let us call it misspeak... if we misspeak before the week is out, we owe the other five dollars."

"Okay, but hows... how about we make it forty bucks?"

"We can do that, but should you lose, that is quite a few weeks without an allowance."

"I'm okay with that."

"When should we start?"

"Hows abouts... about right now?"

"*It's* a deal," Av said, putting out his hand to shake on it.

After the two shook hands and Blue left the car, he paused before closing the door. "Again, what time will you pick us up this afternoon?"

"I will be here at three-thirty."

Blue made a mischievous smile. "Great, and it's *I'll* not *I will*. Please bring my forty bucks when you come to pick us up."

After Blue closed the door, Av drove off laughing a rare belly laugh.

"What was that about? You made him laugh big time."

"I just got him to give us twenty bucks each."

"Seriously?"

"Yes."

"That's too cool! But, hey, next time, try to get him to give us a dog."

"I'll see what I can do, but no promises."

AUTHOR'S NOTES

1) Though the Characters, their situations, and events are fictitious, the named streets, except for Gilmore Street, are true for the period of the story and are described accurately. Carson Street was later named Graystone Drive.

2) All the locations mentioned in Halifax, including the stores, malls, restaurants, cinemas, and even "Cordite Cove", are real as of the period of the story, with the exception of the old graveyard that is a mile and a half away, but as described.

ABOUT THE AUTHOR

Michael Kroft is a Nova Scotian Haligonian and writes character-driven novels about the relationships between complex and lovable characters. Having almost completed his first series, Herring Cove Road, he's now working on his next series, The Lovelys' Family Tree.

Current Works:

The Not-so-Nuclear Family Saga Series, *Herring Cove Road:*

Volume 1) On Herring Cove Road: Mr. Rosen and His 43Lb Anxiety

Volume 2) Still on Herring Cove Road: Hickory, Dickory, Death

Volume 3) Off Herring Cove Road: The Problem Being Blue

Volume 4) Before Herring Cove Road: Ruth Goldman and the Nincompoop

Volume 5) Still Before Herring Cove Road: The War of the Rosens
(Coming June 2024)

The Family Saga Series, *The Lovelys' Family Tree:*

Volume 1) Indentured Bonds: The First Generation, Circa 1715

Volume 2) Family Bonds: The Second Generation, Circa 1735 (Coming January 2024)

Made in United States
Troutdale, OR
06/25/2024

20807968R00141